T0047253

PENGUIN BOOKS
MY MOTHER PATTU

An award-winning writer, Saras Manickam's story, 'My Mother Pattu' won the regional prize for Asia in the 2019 Commonwealth Short Story Contest. In 2021, it was included in the anthology, *The Art and Craft of Asian Stories*, published by Bloomsbury, and in 2022, it was published in *The Best of Malaysian Short Fiction in English 2010–2020*. Saras Manickam worked as a teacher, teacher-trainer, copywriter, Business English trainer, copy-editor, and writer of textbooks, school workbooks and coffee-table books while writing short stories at night. Her various work experiences enabled insights into characters, and life experiences, shaping the authenticity which marks her stories. She also won the 2017 DK Dutt Award for her story, 'Charan'. Some of her other stories have appeared in *Silverfish* and *Readings from Readings* anthologies, while one was shortlisted for the 2021 Masters Review Summer Short Story Award. She lives and works in Kuala Lumpur, Malaysia.

My Mother Pattu

Saras Manickam

PENGUIN BOOKS

An imprint of Penguin Random House

PENGUIN BOOKS

USA | Canada | UK | Ireland | Australia
New Zealand | India | South Africa | China | Southeast Asia

Penguin Books is part of the Penguin Random House group of companies
whose addresses can be found at global.penguinrandomhouse.com

Published by Penguin Random House SEA Pvt. Ltd
9, Changi South Street 3, Level 08-01,
Singapore 486361

First published in Penguin Books by Penguin Random House SEA 2023

Copyright © Saras Manickam 2023

All rights reserved

10 9 8 7 6 5 4 3 2 1

ISBN 9789815058918

Typeset in Garamond by MAP Systems, Bangalore, India

www.penguin.sg

To Senthu
Sharon Bakar
And my writing circle:
Soo Choon Teh, Mercy Thomas, Sharon Ohno
and in loving memory, Leah Ariadne Ray

Contents

1. Number One, Mambang Lane   1

2. Witch Lady   18

3. Dey Raju   33

4. My Mother Pattu   41

5. Charan   53

6. The Princess of Lumut   61

7. Invisible   72

8. It's All Right, Auntie   84

9. Will You Let Him Drink the Wind?   89

10. Woman in the Mirror   93

11. When We Are Young   107

12. When I Speak of Kuala Lumpur   119

13. Cartwheels on the Corridor   133

14. Call It by Its Name   156

Acknowledgements   165

Permissions and Credits   167

1

Number One, Mambang Lane

When I was sixteen, I committed a crime: *I fell in love. I got myself a boyfriend.* Okay, two crimes. In those days in Malaysia, 1964, properly brought up Hindu girls made arranged marriages. Only Christians usually named Rita or Dolly, like the bad girls in Indian movies, fell in love with good Hindu boys and ruined their lives. I had just sat for my Senior Cambridge exam and was waiting for the results. In the meantime, as everyone did those days, I signed up to learn typewriting. While the rest of the students practised 'the quick brown fox jumps over the lazy dog,' I typed love letters to Gopal who sat next to me in class. I had never sat beside a boy in my life.

My mother found three letters from him tucked between the pages of my book *History of Malaya* on my bookshelf. She read them of course. They all began with 'My darling Meena'.

In our Tamil community, dishonour descended equally upon parents and children. However, there was time still to avert discovery as no one else knew about Gopal and me. So, stone-faced and tight-lipped, my mother packed me off to an uncle and his wife whom I hardly knew, who lived in a stupid town with a stupid name. I was given no chance at all to contact my Gopal. I wondered how he would take the loss. In Indian movies, the hero usually took to drink.

That was how I came to live with Uncle Rama and Auntie Sundari in Mambang right in the boondocks of nowhere, as far away as possible from Penang, my hometown and Gopal's. I kept myself aloof. My exile, I wore like a black dog on my shoulders, feeding it with surly defiance.

Mambang Lane was a gravel track that meandered off the main road for a quarter mile before it sloped down to a wooden jetty on the Mambang River. Just before the jetty lay two rows of zinc-roofed housing quarters for town council labourers. Local people called that area, *the Lines*. It came with its own reputation. Apparently, once someone got a bit of education or money, they moved away and never ever admitted that they came from the Lines.

Mambang Lane itself was a motley community of Indians, Chinese, Malays, the odd Eurasian or two. Uncle Rama's house was a sprawling brick with green-and-white bamboo blinds that shaded the porch in the afternoons. Lalli, the half-white, half-Indian girl, lived with her Chinese father and Indian grandmother—I know, I was confused at first too—in a wood-and-brick double-storey house a few doors down the road. Some weekends, her father played mahjong in Auntie Lai's house. Auntie Lai was our immediate neighbour. The games went on for hours deep into the night. When I lay in bed, I listened to the shuffling of the mahjong tiles. I found it oddly comforting.

Mak Enom's Malay house was on stilts. Kitchibhai's family lived in a wooden house with loads of land where his mother reared chickens and planted fruit trees. The witch lady lived in a doll's house with a tin roof.

I didn't notice all these at first, of course. I was steadfast in my isolation on the porch swing. I ignored everyone including Lord Ganesha, the elephant god, who sat at the top of the main door, looking down at me with inscrutable eyes. What did he know about love, celibate elephant-head?

At first, Auntie Sundari and Uncle Rama left me alone—for which I was not sure whether to feel relief or outrage. As a couple, they were not bad looking, though to my eyes, Uncle Rama was ancient at almost forty. His iron-grey hair brushed away from his high forehead. He was pleasant enough to look at until he smiled, then all at once, his face lit up with such sweetness it was almost luminous. He looked like Gregory Peck. I knew Gregory Peck because the Drama Club in my school screened *Roman Holiday* to raise funds.

Auntie Sundari was Uncle Rama's second wife. His first died of TB soon after marriage. Years after her death, he went on holiday to India and came back with a wife fifteen years younger than him. Auntie Sundari was not exactly a beauty so I can't explain why any room felt brighter or happier when she was in it. I suspect it was because she wore lipstick at home. Only fast women, including those named Dolly or Rita wore lipstick in my mother's book. My mother had no idea that I actually owned a lipstick, cleverly hidden in my underwear drawer. Auntie Sundari had liquid black eyes which she lined with kohl. A cluster of diamonds shone softly on her right nostril. Her hair was thick and curly and she wore it the traditional way as a long thick plait that reached below her waist. Sometimes she bunched it into a bun at the nape of her neck. She wore stiff cotton sarees at home. When the sun wilted the starch, the saree clung to her body framing her breasts and hips.

For such an old person, Uncle Rama displayed the most blatant affection towards his wife in public. Uncle Rama tucked strands of jasmine into Auntie Sundari's hair every evening when he came home from work, buying the flowers from the flower-seller outside the temple. Sometimes he bent low to kiss the top of her head, her nape, shoulders until Auntie Sundari laughingly wriggled away. Nights, they sat in the swing, listening to old Tamil songs on the radio. Uncle Rama would drape his arm around his wife's waist and never remove it even if visitors dropped by. Once there was this very old love song on the radio. When it ended, Auntie Sundari turned to Uncle Rama and *kissed him on the lips*. I fell off my chair but luckily, I wasn't hurt. Honestly, I thought only white people kissed on the lips like they did in English movies. I'd never seen Indians behave like that. I mean, my parents never ever touched in public. Their conversations were about the children (my brothers and me); about money (my mother needed to cut down on buying gold); about their relatives (who was getting married and who was ill); and other very proper stuff. My father talked to his friends about politics and business; my mother talked to hers about going to temple, or about problematic maids or why other people's children were so much cleverer than hers.

Uncle Rama and Auntie Sundari talked about all sorts of things as if they were equals. It was bewildering to see how he listened to her opinion as if it mattered. I wasn't used to it. Especially, I couldn't get my head round them laughing together like newly marrieds. I tried to think of any one time when my parents had laughed together for the sheer joy of it, and failed. In Tamil movies, once they were married, the heroine would call her husband, Athan. I loved that Auntie Sundari called him that. I thought it was one of the most romantic words ever and secretly practised saying it. My mother called my father Meena's Appa— what's the romance there, I ask?

We were having tea one evening when I asked Uncle Rama how he met Auntie Sundari. He blushed. For the first time, he hummed and hawed. 'Oh well, it was just one of those things, you know. We met, we liked each other . . . '

Auntie Sundari screamed with laughter. 'Liar!' She beamed at me. 'Let me tell you the story. He came to Chennai on holiday and my brother—who'd been his best friend in college—invited him to stay with us. My parents knew him from before and they really liked him and they wanted him to marry me. You know, arranged marriage and all that. Plus, he would be such a stable influence on me because I was such a wild creature.' She rolled her eyes. 'But he didn't want to marry me. He said no, no, no to my father, to my brother . . . And he said no to me. "No, I cannot marry her. She's too young. She should marry someone younger than me. I'm too old for her. It's not fair to her. So, no, no, I can't marry her. I won't marry her."'

'Really?' I cried. This was just like in the movies; no, it was even better. 'What did you do?'

'I asked him outright whether I was repulsive or something. He said—he said—'Auntie Sundari's voice softened. 'I was like a star in the sky and he wasn't right for me which was why he was going away.'

She gave a little laugh.

'He was about to leave for Bangalore. The car was waiting. The family, neighbours, friends were milling around, waiting to say goodbye. And I went up to him in front of everyone and kissed him. I kissed him on his lips—and his arms went around me and he kissed me back.' She leaned back on her chair, her eyes shining. 'I was a fallen woman. I'd kissed him in front of the world. He had no choice but to marry me.'

I gazed at her with rapture. I'd never kissed anyone, not even my boyfriend. I couldn't wait to find out what it felt like. Uncle Rama leaned across and pushed away a strand of hair from his wife's forehead. 'You were this vibrant thing, completely alive, happy. I had no right to marry you and bring you to this *ulu* town with one single cinema theatre, no concerts, no plays, no bookshop, no library, nothing.'

'That's why, Athan, I want to go back to Chennai to visit,' Auntie Sundari said. 'I haven't been back, not once since I came here.'

The moment she spoke, it was as if the lights dimmed in Uncle Rama's face. I knew then that this conversation was old and repeated.

'You may not come back, Sundari,' he said.

'Of course, I will,' she cried. 'I just want to walk on Marina Beach, munching on sundal and bhaji or even cotton candy. Catch a play or two. And a few concerts. I want to see M.S. Subbulakshmi singing in person instead of listening to her records; walk around town and spend all day at the bookshops. Travel a bit. Lie with my head on my Amma's lap and listen to her stories.' She looked at him. 'Then, I'll come back.'

He shook his head. 'I don't know how to live without you anymore.'

Auntie Sundari closed her eyes. 'We can go together, or I can go alone. I just want to go back home for a few weeks. That's all I'm asking.'

I expected Auntie Sundari to be petulant and not speak to anybody later that evening; I was wrong. She behaved as usual, perhaps with a touch of sadness. She couldn't carry anger for long.

* * *

Two weeks into my forced exile, I woke up to what was now the familiar. Uncle Rama put an M.S. Subbulakshmi record on the turntable and turned up the volume. The singer's fluid voice filled the creases of the waking house as I plucked flowers for the altar. Prayers over, Uncle Rama placed a red pottu on Auntie Sundari's forehead. His hand lingered on her face; his eyes gleamed whenever they settled on her, getting an impish grin from her.

Afterwards, she sat on the Indian rug in the sitting room, tuning her harmonium, waiting for her students. She taught classical Indian singing. This was a genteel house. It was becoming harder to hold on to memories of my boyfriend. We had after all, just the three letters between us and twice, he'd held my hand.

At eight, Sita of the short blouse arrived. Our house was the first stop in her rounds in Mambang Lane where she worked as a maid at a number of houses.

Sita wore gilt loops in her ears and flowers in her hair, flowers plucked in passing from someone's garden. Her blouse, tight-fitting and moulded to her body, exposed her midriff. A thin cotton cloth covered the front of her blouse, one end tucked into her waist, the other flung over her shoulder. When she bent to sweep or mop, her breasts strained and thrust and threatened to pop open the buttons. Her bangles tinkled and clashed. Her sarongs were loud. Now and then, she stopped to loosen and retie her sarong, shaking it first. She always made such a drama of it. Sita sang snatches of the latest Tamil love songs as she worked. At times, when she sang with too much enthusiasm, it interfered with Auntie Sundari's classes.

If Uncle Rama was having his breakfast, Sita started a conversation with him. Always courteous, Uncle Rama listened, responded and occasionally, he laughed.

When this happened, the harmonium in the sitting room fell silent. Auntie Sundari bustled into the dining hall, with a glare for Sita. Uncle Rama, he never noticed anything.

Each day, Sita had a story or two to tell about her family. I was an avid fan of her stories for she lived in the Lines where grubby, half-naked children played on the dirt patch outside their grim, perpetually dark homes. In the Lines, women chattered loudly. When they went out, they dressed in parrot-green, shocking pink or gaudy red, sometimes all at once. There were noisy quarrels and drunken fights especially at the end of each month when the men received their wages. It was a world of squalor, vulgarity, far removed from mine. I found it entrancing and wished Sita would invite me to her house so I could step inside their lives, but she never did.

Sita shared her home with her father, his current woman and various children, not all of whom were her siblings. She shrugged when I asked where her mother was. Her father's subsequent 'wives' had all run away as well. He was between 'wives' at the moment. I used to see him every Friday when he came to collect Sita's wages. Auntie Sundari kept back a portion for Sita's personal use. This led to polite entreaties to hand over the entire sum. His mother had just died (apparently she died with great regularity every few months). He needed the money for funeral expenses. Or he had to go to the big hospital in Kuala Lumpur to have an operation on his left leg. See, he could barely walk. Or he needed to buy a gold chain for Sita—saving up for her wedding, he was. Always, his voice was subservient, whining. An insignificant, small man in stained baggy shorts. I wondered what attracted the women to him.

'Get away from this town, Sita,' Auntie Sundari told Sita. 'Get out of your father's clutches.'

'Get away? Where? And do what?'

Auntie Sundari sighed. 'Look at you—you can read and write. You can speak English. Go away somewhere else, become a clinic nurse or something.'

'Fine for you to talk, Sundari Akka. You're married to the nicest man in this town.'

'Get married then, you silly girl.'

Sita's face darkened. 'Who will marry me, Akka? Only someone like my father. Someone who collects my wages and beats me and gives me half a dozen brats to keep me down.'

Auntie Sundari snorted. 'That's why I'm telling you to get away from here, girl. Get away from your father, from this life. Keep your money for yourself. And stop complaining for a change.'

Sita was stung. 'Sure, I could. If I had a husband like yours, I'd be singing the same song too, and giving everybody free advice.'

It struck me even then, that Sita was always deliberately rude to Auntie Sundari. Even the way she called her Akka, sister, dripped with scorn. I didn't know how she was allowed to get away with it. Perhaps it was because they were both about the same age. Auntie Sundari, at twenty-four, was barely a year older than Sita and married for five years already. Still, my mother would have kicked out any maid who gave her the slightest lip.

'I can write an entire cinema story on men, you know,' Sita said with the weight of knowledge heavy in her voice. I sniggered. Even I knew that Sita's take on her men-friends was from Tamil film dialogues, freely borrowed. 'They flit about me, moths to the flame. Can't help themselves.'

'Then choose one of them, silly girl. I don't believe a word you say, you're such a liar.'

'I told you they don't want me for marriage, Akka!' Sita squealed. 'I'm from the Lines, remember? Who wants me for marriage? They are all married men, anyway. Fat men, thin men, bald men, hairy men . . . They rub their hands and give me little presents and they grope and try their luck.' Her voice dropped. 'Of course, if they were rich like your husband . . . '

'Oh, shut up girl!'

I didn't know it then but Sita fed us her stories bit by bit, baiting us with morsels that began to scald Auntie Sundari. One day, from unnamed men, all crazy for her, she began to mention just the one man. 'Older than me, he is, but when I see him, my knees go all weak, you know what I mean?' she said to no one in particular. 'Like that actor, that 007 something—what's his name?'

'James Bond,' I replied promptly. Auntie Sundari sighed.

Sita nodded. 'Yes, James Bond. When I meet him, I'm like, "Take me! Take me!" No, don't you snort, Akka. God's truth. That's how I feel. He's not offering marriage, of course, but my father, he says, think of the money, girl. All that glorious money.'

'Doesn't he have a wife, children?' Auntie Sundari said as she shoved pots into the cupboard.

'Akka, you'll break the clay pot,' Sita said, making no effort to rescue the pot. 'They're all married at that age, the men. What to do? But she hasn't given him any children, that's the rub. I could give him children. Many children.' She dismissed the hapless wife, arching her neck to reveal the taut curves of her body.

Auntie Sundari looked exasperated. 'You stupid girl. You think men are crazy about you? You . . . you . . . it's all in your mind.'

Sita turned to look at her. Her words were sly. 'You think I'm trash, don't you? A girl from the Lines. Just wait. I can't tell you his name . . . not yet. One day, you will know.'

'I don't want to know, okay? Just do your work and go away.' Auntie Sundari left the kitchen abruptly. I found her in the prayer room clutching a statue of Lord Murugan to her breast. Her eyes were shut tight. The sight was familiar. I had seen it twice in Tamil films.

'Sita's being mischievous. If she's upsetting you, just sack her.'

Auntie Sundari shook her head. 'How can I throw sand on her rice bowl, Meena? That wretched girl needs the money. Think of all the beatings she escapes because I give her wages to her father. And we pay almost double what the neighbours pay.'

* * *

Some mornings, when Auntie Sundari made thosai with sambar and chutney, Kitchibhai joined us for breakfast. Kitchibhai, whose real name was Ranjit Singh (nobody including his parents ever called him that) was our local thug. He wore his hair in a knot on top of his head, wrapping it with a strip of coloured cloth, sometimes green, sometimes white, sometimes vermilion. Tendrils escaped down the nape of his neck. Kitchibhai only wore a turban if it was a special occasion.

He was born in Mambang Lane, a fat, happy baby who grew up into a cute child who became a wild teen gang member. Rumour was, he spent some years as His Majesty's guest but no one would ever confirm it. Kitchi felt a fierce protectiveness towards the people of Mambang Lane. They were his tribe. He watched out for them and in turn, most of them watched out for him.

The first time I met him, he said, 'Meena, if any fellow tries to be funny with you, you tell him you are Kitchibhai's sister.'

When Kitchi was sixteen, the carnival came to town with its star attraction, the ronggeng girls. Games stalls, food stalls, a merry-go-round, a Big Wheel, but Kitchi had eyes only for the ronggeng girls, red-lipped dancing sirens in their see-through embroidered kebayas and tight batik sarongs. Perched on gilt chairs on a stage in the middle of the public field, they pouted at the crowd. Men paid for tickets, then went up on stage for a dance with a girl of their choice.

Even as the men scrambled for dance tickets, Kitchi threw his money at the startled ticket seller and sprinted up the steps. He grabbed the prettiest girl and as the band began to play, Kitchi danced. He did not know the steps. It didn't matter. He imitated the girl's movements, added some Bollywood moves, and then some Bhangra for good measure. Dance after dance after dance, Kitchi remained on stage, with a wide, blissful smile on his face.

Someone told his father. The old man, brandishing a walking stick, hurried to the town field. Word spread that Kitchibhai's father was coming. A murmur rose among the spectators. 'Kitchibhai! Kitchibhai! Your father is coming!' Kitchi heard nothing. His entire body and mind were riveted in the moment. The crowd murmured louder and louder, but still he danced. In desperation, Auntie Sundari, newly married and barely a few years older than him, hitched up her saree and raced up the stage and yanked at him, roaring, 'Kitchi! Kitchibhai! Your father is coming!'

When Kitchibhai related the story at breakfast, we burst into laughter. I noticed Auntie Sundari's hand on Kitchi's shoulder. Sita entered the room at that moment. Seeing Kitchi, she turned around and scuttled away. He told Uncle Rama, 'That girl is no good. She'll create trouble. Let her go.'

Uncle Rama shook his head, 'Go where? Do what? Poor girl. She means no harm, Kitchi. If only there is something we can do . . . ' Spell broken; the softness left Auntie Sundari's face. She pressed Kitchi's shoulder. He lay his hand on hers.

I thought it odd that Auntie Sundari was always touchy-feely with Kitchibhai but then where I came from, my father never touched me, affectionately or otherwise. So, what did I know? Besides, Uncle Rama never seemed to mind.

* * *

That Friday, Sita came to work more than two hours late without any explanation. She was sullen. There were no snatches of song, no drama with her sarong. She thumped the broom; she sloshed the water on the floor as she mopped. She ignored me. She even sniffed and turned away when she saw Uncle Rama having a late coffee in the dining room. I thought he might say something but he didn't. He was looking at Sita with a strange expression, as if he were seeing her with new eyes.

Sita was even more abrupt than usual with Auntie Sundari. I could see Auntie barely holding it together. She was teary-eyed that day. She'd received a long letter from her family in the post that morning. Her youngest brother, Hari, was going to university in England in a few months' time. Could she come visit and say goodbye? They hadn't seen her for almost five years.

Auntie Sundari laughed and cried when she read the letter. 'My little brother is going to the university? I can't believe it. This imp used to tease us with riddles all the time.'

'Really?' I said. 'I love riddles.'

'Hari did too,' she smiled. 'He was always on the look out for new ones. Even when we were waiting to board the ship to come here, and there was all this loving and hugging and kissing, he had to ask us a riddle!'

'What was it? You remember it?'

'I remember everything. Here goes: The words jail and prison mean exactly the same. What do you add to these words to make them opposites? Do you know, Meena?'

'I don't. What do you add?'

She grinned. 'It's so clever. You add -er to them so jailer becomes the opposite of prisoner.' She turned to Uncle Rama, the letter in her hand. 'Athan—I must go back to India to see my brother.'

'Let's talk about it this evening, Sundari.' His voice was bleak.

Sita walked past, carrying a bundle of clothes to wash at the tap outside the kitchen, in the back of the house. Uncle Rama watched her go and then he murmured, 'Poor girl. Sundari, we have to do something for her. She's teetering on the brink . . . marriage is the best, I think.'

'What? Wait a minute.' I'd never heard Auntie Sundari raise her voice before. 'You can see that our maid is teetering on the brink of what I don't know but you can't see your wife doing exactly that? What's the matter with you?'

Uncle Rama blanched. 'I have to tell you about Sita. I met her last night. She . . . this can't go on . . . ' He was about to say more when he jumped up. 'I completely forgot. I have a meeting with the bank manager in twenty minutes. I'd better take the car.' He seemed relieved. 'Tonight, when I come back, we will talk.' He didn't wait for her reply.

She said nothing at first, after he left. She stood there in the middle of the room, stiff as a board. I went to the dining table and poured myself a tumbler of coffee, not caring that it was no longer hot.

'I didn't want to marry him at first; have I told you that?' she whispered, not looking at me. She wasn't looking at anything; she seemed to have gone inside of herself. 'I was in my second year of college, happy; I had dreams. First my degree, then postgraduate. Perhaps in another country.'

'Far out!' I breathed. 'You went to college! I never knew that.'

Auntie Sundari didn't hear me. 'When he came to visit, I knew what they were planning, my parents, my brother. They'd always liked him. I was all ready to say no—except he said it first. "No, no, no," he said, beating me to it.' She laughed. It wasn't a happy sound. 'He kept saying it. I felt insulted, as if I wasn't good enough. It made me look at him, really look at him. I saw how funny he was. And decent. He was truly a good person. How he treated everyone the same, even the maids, the gardeners. He was lovely to me too—we could talk and laugh and disagree. It was fun but all the time, he kept this distance from me. A separateness. He wasn't my friend or my brother. I realized I didn't want him to be any of that either.'

She sat down next to me, placing her hands flat on the table. 'I should have stepped back and thought a bit. I mean, he kept telling me all about his life here—that it was no life, not for me. He told me but I was past listening.'

'Auntie Sundari' I began, without knowing what to say.

She looked at me. 'I have no money, no means. I'll never be able to leave.' There were no tears, no wringing of hands. Her eyes glittered. Auntie Sundari shone, triumphant with despair.

I had never seen her like this. The air in the room weighed me down all of a sudden. My chest constricted. There was no talking to her. Besides, I didn't know how. I crept away to sit on the swing on the porch. It groaned a bit. The creaking was comforting. I saw Kitchibhai striding past. I called to him.

When he entered the house, Auntie Sundari stood up. She was stone calm. 'Kitchi,' she said. He went to her. In one fluid sudden movement, her hands moved to Kitchibhai's head. She drew him close and she kissed him on the lips.

It seemed to last forever when all at once, Kitchibhai was pushing her away, wiping his mouth and saying, 'What the heck . . . Auntie!'

I saw the look on her face—her eyes were opaque, all blood drained from her face. 'Tell your Uncle Rama I kissed you. Tell him!'

Kitchibhai turned to me. I began to blabber. 'It's Uncle Rama. He said they should get Sita married—or maybe he said he wants to marry her . . . I forget.'

Auntie Sundari sighed and said something that choked up her voice. It sounded like 'You idiot'.

'Sita?' Kitchibhai asked me.

I nodded.

He called, 'Sita.' He didn't raise his voice. Within seconds Sita was at the door. She kept shifting on her feet. She didn't look at Auntie Sundari.

'Tell Auntie what happened. Between you and Uncle Rama.'

'Nothing, Kitchibhai! What is this . . . I have no idea what you're saying . . . ' Her voice wheedled. I realized with a start that she sounded just like her father.

'The truth.' His voice was ice. 'I was there.'

A chill shot through my body at the menace in his voice. It dawned on me then that he *was* a thug. He drew up a chair and sat on it, one ankle crossed on the other knee, his hands stretched out on his legs. He fastened his eyes on Sita and held her gaze. She couldn't turn away.

Her voice was dull, without emotion. 'I know in the evenings when he walks home, he takes the short cut past the vacant shop next to the football field. I have seen him many times. Some days, I wait and then walk by the shop, pretending I'm on my way to town. He always greets me. Asks ever so politely how I am. I've never met anyone like him. When he talks to me, I feel special, like I'm a lady. You don't know how that feels, to be treated the same as rich or educated people.

'So yesterday, he walked by the shop. I stopped him. He smiled as he always did and then I—I said, all in a rush, for I was suddenly nervous and shy, I said I wanted to be his woman. That I loved him . . . and I would make him very happy. I would please him, do anything, anything at all he wanted. I reached out to touch him . . . he stepped back. He . . . he said ever so kindly, "Don't. I'm married. You know that." Hah.'

Sita gave a strangled laugh. The sound echoed hollow and empty around the room. No one said a word. She looked at Auntie Sundari and her voice cracked just a bit.

'I told him I was young, strong. He shook his head and began to walk away. I ran to him. Look, I can give you children, I said. He looked me in the eyes then—it made me feel—I can't explain—he wasn't angry or anything, but I felt he didn't really see me at all. He—he said, "Sundari is not just my wife. Sundari's the woman I want." It was as if you and he were in a circle by yourselves and that was enough for him. I was invisible.'

Sita turned to Kitchibhai. 'I wore my newest Deepavali saree. Orange with a red border. Japanese nylex, you know. Cost me twenty-five dollars. Lipstick. Rouge. Painted my nails.' She shook her head. 'He didn't even notice. Where were you? Inside the shop? I was waiting half an hour before he came. I never saw you.'

'I wasn't there.'

'But you said . . . '

'I said I was there because I *know* Uncle Rama.'

When Sita left the room, Auntie Sundari walked to a large mirror on the wall, overlooking the dining table. She stared at her image. 'You must tell him what I did, Kitchi,' she said. 'You have to.'

'I can't, how can I? That's my Uncle Rama, dammit.'

'You must.'

'No. I don't know why you did it, Auntie, but I'm never telling him.'

Auntie Sundari sat for a while after Kitchibhai went away. A little later, she got up, took something from a drawer and headed for the kitchen. I followed, not knowing what else to do. Sita was sitting at the table with her head in her hands. Auntie Sundari placed Sita's wages on the table. 'Take this before your father comes. You . . . you can still work here if you want.'

Sita looked up. She eased herself from her chair, her eyes never leaving my Auntie. 'Don't. I don't need your bloody kindness.' She flicked at Auntie Sundari with a contemptuous hand. 'When he said, "Sundari's the woman I want", I knew I'd lost. How could I compete?'

Auntie Sundari shook her head. 'There was no competition, Sita. There never was.'

'You're lying! I know you're lying! I strung you along, didn't I? Made you believe everything I said?'

Auntie Sundari shook her head again. 'No. You never did. You kept creating a fantasy that could never come true.' She looked weary all of a sudden. 'You fool. That's why I kept telling you to go away, to have a chance at a new life.'

'Why do you keep lying?' Sita screamed. She gathered her things and as she walked out the kitchen door, she was still howling. 'I tricked her. I know I did.' Her voice wound its way back to us as she walked out to the driveway and out the main gate. 'Why is she so lucky? Why am I forever the outsider?'

Auntie Sundari sat in the kitchen for a long time. When she finally began to cry, she made no sound. I sat down at the table. I couldn't talk. The only thing on my mind was her brother telling her riddles one laughing, loving day when her family had waved her goodbye.

END

2

Witch Lady

Witch Lady lived in a wooden cottage with a tin roof; in the porch, a metal swing with rusty arms creaked forlorn noises. Lalang and other sundry weeds fought for space alongside marigolds on their straggly stems, jasmines and hibiscus in the patch of earth in front of the house. Faded dirty blue paint peeled from its walls, revealing wood bleached white by the sun. Its window shutters didn't close properly and the drainpipe that ran down from the roof constantly dripped water. It appeared an oversized doll's house, long abandoned by its owner.

Except, it wasn't abandoned. I had seen the lady who lived there. She was always immaculate, sometimes wearing a crisp cotton dress, freshly starched; sometimes draped in an old-fashioned silk saree. She would stand in her porch for a moment looking bemused at the world before her. Sometimes, she glided past our house, looking at our open windows, open door, an aloof, secret smile on her face. Sometimes, she chatted with Auntie Sundari. Just once, when I was with Auntie Sundari, I turned around and caught her peering closely at me, a curious moment during which I felt stripped of all privacy, with my secrets revealed for her to read.

I called her 'Auntie' as I did most of the other women in the neighbourhood. The women with children were easy to address.

I just said Kitchibhai's Amma, Salmiah's Mak or Seng Chye's Ma and that was enough. They didn't carry their own names, these women, only the label of being their children's mothers. But this lady whose name I did not know, I gave her a name. I called her 'Witch Lady,' beautiful young-old witch with the white hair.

One evening, soon after I arrived at Mambang Lane for my long exile, Auntie Sundari thrust a tiffin carrier of idlis, sambar and coconut chutney into my hands. 'Meena, take this to the Auntie at Number Six. She loves idlis.'

At that time, I wasn't yet talking to anybody, my uncle and aunt included. I was still feeling hard done by at being sent away to Mambang, just because I'd fallen in love. Was that such a crime? How ridiculous it was. I had not forgiven anybody and I wasn't talking to anyone either, but this was different. I took the tiffin carrier eagerly. I was finally going to see the inside of the Witch Lady's house.

I stepped into the porch of the doll's house and knocked on the door before, too late, my ears registered a low keening like that of an animal in pain, followed by a wave of weeping. I didn't know what to do. I wanted to get away, but my feet seemed stuck to the porch floor.

Presently, the crying stopped. The door opened. For a moment, I couldn't recognize the Witch Lady. Bloodshot eyes glared at me from a puffy face. Her cheeks appeared damp with tears. She wiped them away with her sleeve. I noticed the tear at the armpit that reached down the side seam.

We stood looking at each other. 'Meena,' she said finally and looked at the tiffin carrier that I held in front of me. I didn't say a word. I didn't know what to say. She closed her eyes and scrunched up her face. A moment later, eyes wide open and a huge smile pasted on her lips, she said, 'Sundari's idlis?'

I couldn't believe it. One moment she had been weeping—I'd heard her—and the next—it was like makeover magic in front of my eyes. 'Yes. With sambar and coconut chutney.'

She smiled again, this time with genuine pleasure. 'Dear Sundari's idlis. The fluffiest, softest . . . ' She didn't take the carrier from me. Instead, she opened the door wide enough for me to enter. I hesitated.

'I'm not coming in, Auntie. I have to go.'

'Enter.'

I entered. I handed her the container of food. She finally took it and placing it on a table, she took a packet of cigarettes from her pocket. She removed a cigarette and lit it, inhaling deeply. I tried to look nonchalant as if I was always hanging around women who smoked. In Tamil films those days, it was always the nightclub dancer, usually called Dolly or Rita, who smoked. Witch Lady exhaled and grinned at me, her tears forgotten.

'Only bad women smoke, eh? And loose Christian women?'

I gulped.

'How old are you child? Fifteen?'

'Sixteen,' I whispered.

'Ever been in love?' She threw the question out casually as she flicked the ashes off her cigarette. My cheeks burned. I remembered my beloved Gopal, who had held my hand twice and had written me three love letters. I remembered how that dreadful sin of falling in love banished me from my boyfriend, from my scandalized parents, from my typing class, to this nowhere town of strangers, my aunt and uncle included. I didn't want to think about it anymore, so I looked around the room instead.

I was in the tiniest hall with two bedrooms to the left and at the back, a soot-stained kitchen. The kitchen was unlit but there was enough natural light to see a pile of unwashed dishes in the sink. A stove sat on a raised concrete slab. Under the slab was a pile of chopped wood. Witch Lady was still using firewood for cooking, while my Auntie Sundari had already moved on to kerosene. I felt a little superior.

Inside the hall, on one low wall, hung picture upon fading picture, studio portraits of a single woman in various poses. How she made love to the camera, I thought, posing this way and that. Every photograph was different save for the expression in her eyes. They were hungry. I knew the woman. It was Witch Lady.

'Judith! You are looking at Judith!' I spun around. Witch Lady's face was contorted. She stubbed out her cigarette, grinding it down onto an ashtray already overflowing with stale stubs. 'Nobody ever saw me. It was Judith, Judith, Judith all the time. Bloody, fucking Judith.' She grabbed the nearest photograph and smashed it on the windowsill. Fragments scattered on the sill and the ground outside. A stream of Tamil spewed from her lips. I didn't understand half the words, hadn't heard half of them before but I guessed they were foul. My parents never swore. Her rage alarmed me and I was afraid. I edged towards the door but even in my fear, the words fascinated me and I wished she'd speak more slowly so I could pick up a phrase or two.

'You can't leave.' Witch Lady reached the door before I could and slammed it shut. Her body drooped; her voice turned dull. She was not looking at me. 'You can't leave before you listen to my story. Everyone must know the-truth-of-what-actually-happened-between-Judith-and-me.'

'Er . . . I don't know who Judith is. I don't know you. I don't want to know. Honest. I have to go now. There's a Tamil film tonight on TV.'

I could have spoken in Swahili for all that she listened to me. Lighting another cigarette, she shuffled to the windowsill, uncaring of the glass fragments. 'I must start at the beginning; when the British came back, and all those Europeans, after the war. All the important people were white—estate managers, company managers, important lawyers, doctors. Everyone who mattered,' she shrugged, 'to us at any rate. The beginning of my story—that was what 1950? Fourteen years ago—bloody hell it's been that long already? So, the beginning—got to start with the bloody parents, don't I? Agnes and Milton Smith. Indian-Anglican, claiming to be Anglo-Indian because of our English surname. Better Anglo than bloody Indian, you know?'

Bloody Indian? I thought how outraged my parents would be at this. They were always going on and on about our glorious civilization, our culture, music, dance, song, literature. Not that they let me learn music and dance. They were too conservative for that. 'What do you mean? Being Indian is no good?' I asked. 'Our civilization is ancient, Auntie. Thousands of years of music, poetry, dance, literature—in case you've forgotten.'

She waved away my outrage. 'Girl—you can have thousands of years, no, ten thousand years of bloody civilization, if you like. It's all no use. In this country, you're coolies and rubber-tappers and labourers. That's all you are. Fat lot of good your civilization does here. Drunken fellows. Wife-beaters. That's you Indians.'

'No, Auntie,' I was earnest. 'Not every Indian is a rubber-tapper. We're doctors, you know, and teachers, and lawyers and railway station managers . . . why are you looking at me like that?' my voice trailed off.

Witch Lady leaned towards me until her nose was just inches from my face. She waved her cigarette at me. 'Just checking to see how big a fool you are, you silly child. The best Indian doctor is just one doctor among all the rubber-tappers, and labourers and railway workers, etcetera, etcetera. The fairest Indian will always be the blackest fellow among everyone else. Face it.

'So, which Indian Christian wants to be a black Indian when they can pass for an Anglo? English name, English dress, English perks and maybe English husband . . . ' She took a long drag on her cigarette. 'Of course, we were Indian in the inside where nobody could see us—I mean where no white man could see us. Indian as anything, ha—mutton curry, chicken varuval. Thosai, idli. Salt fish sambal. My father needed his Indian food, Indian movies, Tamil songs.'

She got up and switched on the lone electric bulb in the room. It cast dappled light on to the table and chairs. Dark shadows retreated to the wall of photographs. Trapped in the dark, the pictures sulked.

She seemed unaware of the creeping night, of me, of the now rapidly cooling idlis in the tiffin carrier. As she spoke, I realized the past had sneaked into the room, a seamless breeze sweeping in from the window, down the chimney and up from the floor. I was half fearful, half in thrall. This was better than any Tamil movie.

* * *

Late nights, Agnes and Milton sat on the swing in the porch, swilling beer, smoking Craven A cigarettes and brawling, usually about money and Milton's inability to earn more as a mere clerk in a law office. The money wasn't enough to keep him in the style he wanted. With each successive beer, their voices got higher, louder, more raucous. Inevitably, the weeping came next, usually from Agnes, followed by one tentative giggle, then another and another, before they started cuddling and moved off to bed. The dramas of Agnes and Milton always took place on the swing, with neighbours pretending not to see or hear, with the daughters cringing inside the house. And so, the years passed. Agnes and Milton remained poor, but they had one trump card. Their daughter Judith.

'Of course, they had two daughters, Judith and me, Millie, but I was too dark. Not clever enough either. Look here, Meena, do you think I'm dark?' Millie appealed, stretching her hand out at me. I told her she was rather fair. She nodded, pleased.

'Judith hated being poor. It was like being trapped in some bloody nightmare. So, all her life, she wanted out. In school, she made friends with rich girls, Anglo girls and even the one or two English girls so she could visit their homes, meet their parents, their friends, *their brothers*. Oh, she could ingratiate. And she watched and learned how the beautiful rich moved, talked, sat, behaved. Back home, it was hours upon hours of practice. Perfecting a low, breathless voice, sashaying into a room, languid movements . . . She fashioned a new Judith whom she could put on like a dress.'

'She pretended to be someone else?'

Millie sighed her annoyance at me loudly. 'It was never a game with her. It was survival. I mean, what else could you do? Our lives were all about marriage, marriage to the right man.'

'I'm never going to get married,' I said, thinking of my lost love. 'I'll get a job and a dog and a car and I'll be perfectly happy.'

Millie made a rude sound with her mouth. 'You silly fool. Those days, we had to get married. What else could we do? No money, no education.'

'That can't be true, I mean . . . ' I started to speak but Millie gave me a look that threatened painful death. I shut up. As I listened to her story, it occurred to me what a natural storyteller she was. It didn't occur to me at all that it sounded rehearsed.

'Judith decided she wanted a white husband. Love comes easy when it's a white man, you know that? Mum and Dad encouraged her. She was their passport. I—Millie—was ignored. Millie wasn't pretty enough, not smart. It was always only Judith.' Millie stopped and blew her nose on a handkerchief she dug out of her dress pocket.

'You must have hated her.' My voice broke into the silence, a nail scratching on a blackboard. For a moment she was still. Then with a look of disbelief, she cried, 'Hated? Are you crazy, girl? Why, she was my sister. I loved her. I was her confidante. Alone with me, only me, Judith could drop the act. No need to pretend because . . . because Millie would never tell. So, what if Judith bullied me or hit me? What if she borrowed my clothes, stole my money from my purse? Afterwards, she always said, "Forgive me, Millie, please? Pretty please?" And Millie always did. Because Millie loved you, you selfish, scheming bitch!' Her voice rose to a cry.

I remembered the smashed photograph, and the festering resentment in Millie's foul language. I remembered to say nothing.

* * *

That long-ago-summer, Judith was in a fever, nerves taut and stretched. Nothing had worked out despite all her cunning. The white planters and officers she cultivated enjoyed the pursuit, but were reluctant to commit. Judith wanted marriage. That was too high a price. She was twenty-five years old. Her parents were getting tetchy. She had been out with too many men. Rumour was she was 'easy'. Judith was frantic. She didn't know what it was that she was doing wrong. It was in that desperate time that she first set eyes on the Englishman, Niles Barrington.

Niles was new to town. Judith never said how they met or what he did for a living. But the moment she saw him, Judith fell head over heels.

She became secretive. She didn't tell her parents about him. She wouldn't let Millie meet him. Millie once secretly followed her sister so she knew where Niles lived, in a small colonial bungalow on Crown Road, a mere fifteen minutes' walk from their home. Evening after evening, Judith slipped away, disappearing for hours, coming home glowing and rapturous. Deep in the night, in their room, she whispered coy remarks into Millie's ears.

'I'll wear a white wedding gown, Millie, with white gloves, a long lace veil trailing behind me. I will be an Englishwoman!'

This went on for weeks until late one night, Judith crept home to their room. Millie woke up to see her sister sitting at the edge of her bed, eyes streaming, mouth stuffed with her scarf to muffle her sobs so her parents wouldn't hear. She was incoherent but Millie finally understood that Niles didn't want to see Judith anymore. It was finished, all over, he'd said. He didn't want to talk about it. He wouldn't explain anything. But he would always remember Judith as the nicest girl he'd ever met. 'Millie, he pushed a wad of notes into my bag and . . . and . . . said thank you . . . and he asked me to leave. How could I leave him? He was my life. My future. I clung to him. I begged him. He . . . he pushed me away.'

All night, Judith wept, sitting hunched on her bed. When she finally dozed into a fitful sleep, Millie counted the money in Judith's handbag. It was $500. She had never seen so much money; even her father didn't earn that much in a month.

Early morning, she woke up to Judith crooning softly as she moved around the room. 'It's all right, Niles, my darling, I forgive you. We'll forget everything you said, all right? We'll forget that you shoved me—oh Niles, bad, bad boy. We'll get married quickly. I'll wear a silk wedding gown and lace gloves and lace veil, and I'll be the most beautiful bride ever, and I'll be all yours, darling. You'll see.'

'What are you doing, Judith?'

'Hush, Millie. Go back to sleep. It's all right. I'm going to Niles now. It's going to be fine. Really.'

Millie groaned. 'Judith, please. It's six in the morning, it's too early.'

'Keep your bloody voice down, Millie.' The next second, Judith was gone.

She's just gone to the bathroom, Millie told herself. She's not actually gone. The minutes passed but Judith did not return. With a start, Millie scrambled out of bed, jumped into her street clothes and raced out to Niles' house.

Streetlights were still shining. The roads were awakening gradually. Millie noticed nothing. She had to get Judith back before anyone noticed she was gone.

Here, Millie stopped and sniffed. She looked pitifully at me. 'I can't continue, Meena. It makes me cry.'

I was too deep into the story; I needed to know what happened next. It took me a while to persuade her to continue. For a moment, her lips parted into a smile. I saw it but it was a fleeting thing. It didn't register in my consciousness.

Millie sped to Niles' house. Judith and a white man were on the veranda of the house. The main door was shut, the windows shuttered. She saw Judith on her knees banging on the front door. Niles was behind her, trying to lift her up. She kept banging at the door as if she wanted to get in. Niles wouldn't let her. She turned and grabbed his leg. He couldn't shift her. 'For God's sake, Judith,' he begged, 'Get up. Get up and leave. Please.'

'Why, Nilesy baby, why?' she wailed. 'You love me—you said so. You said we'd get married.' Judith's face was blotched, her voice weepy and petulant. There was no sign of the crooning, happy Judith of barely an hour before. This woman appeared almost in a trance. Nothing the man said seemed to penetrate her mind. Her dress was torn; it rode up her legs, exposing her upper thighs. Neither Niles nor Judith seemed to notice.

Millie ran to them, calling, 'Judith! Judith!' She didn't seem to hear her. Niles managed to get Judith to stand up. He gripped her face forcing her to look at him. 'Listen, I never told you I loved you. I told you I was married. I never lied to you. The wife is coming out from England this week. I told you already. Leave. Please, Judith.' He turned to Millie, his face mottled with fear and embarrassment. 'Are you the sister? Thank God. Get her out, for heaven's sake. She's causing a bloody scene.'

Millie tried to pull Judith away. She shrugged off Millie's hands and clung to Niles. He pushed her away. She crawled back in a blink and grabbed him again. 'You said she was not a patch on me. That I was the most beautiful woman, most understanding woman in the world. Niles, leave her. You leave her and marry me. Niles. You promised!'

'I never said that, Judith!' Niles was almost beside himself. 'I never said any of that. I told you I was married. I told you.' Despite the cool of the morning, Niles's face was red with fat beads of sweat rolling down his face. Judith's grip on him must have been like iron. He couldn't dislodge her. Millie felt the current of fear that swept through him. With a loud curse, he shoved Judith off so hard, she fell sideways with a thud.

'Go! Just go, Judith.' Breathing heavily, Niles backed into the house, slamming the door so hard, it shook. He opened it slightly immediately. 'You were my good time girl, that was all. If you ever come back here again, if you ever cause trouble, so help me God, I'm calling the police.' He banged the door shut. Judith stared at it for a long time, all fight gone from her body.

Millie paused. She didn't look at me. I don't think she was even aware of me. She was in another world, remembering. 'I can't tell you much about our journey home. Nothing was as it seemed. Judith leaned on me as I half carried, half dragged her along. She was mumbling, "I'm Judith Smith, soon to be Judith Barrington. So nice to meet you. What a delightful pleasure. You are the first to know—I'm getting married . . . you may know my fiancé, Niles. Niles Barrington . . . white silk gown and lace gloves and a lace veil . . . " Over and over again.

'I ached for my sister. All her life, Judith had been primed for nothing else but to catch the right man, the right white man who'd boost our family fortunes, our status. All her energies had been devoted to equipping herself with the most suitable skills to getting this. When Niles appeared in her life, he slipped perfectly into becoming Mr Right. Wittingly or unwittingly, I didn't know. He wasn't even good looking.'

As the sisters made their way home, the morning was coming to life; children were walking to school, some were cycling. The earliest trishaws were already out on the streets, ferrying women from their homes. They were carrying schoolteachers in prim skirts or sarong kebaya, instantly recognisable by the books they carried. Others ferried middle-aged Indian aunties in sarees, Chinese aunties in dresses or samfoo; Malay aunties in their baju kurung, all off to the market, carrying large empty bamboo baskets. Passers-by gave the two girls curious glances. Judith was still talking to herself. Her dress was torn, her bruises were beginning to appear. Their Dad, Mum would be up already. The neighbours would be about. What would happen now? What could she say to them? What would they say? What would happen to Judith? Millie's heart began to race; her head was a mess. She couldn't think ahead.

'Just before we neared our lane, Judith stopped. She took a deep breath. "Wait, Millie." She closed her eyes and scrunched up her face. She breathed deeply. When she opened her eyes, she gave me a watery smile. "Say you forgive me, Millie. Say it." Her voice was firm.

"What are you saying, Judith? Forgive you for what?"

"For everything, Millie. For all the bloody things."

"I don't understand."

"For God's sake, Millie, just say it. Just tell me you forgive me."

"Okay."

"No, you've got to say it. Say it!"

'I must have seemed like a witless fool, Meena,' Millie said. 'I think I was. I really was. Judith sighed and held my face with her hands. "I love you, Millie, I always have. You've always there for me. Despite all the stuff I've done to you, you've always been there." She looked at me earnestly. "That's why I need you to say it."

'She looked like she was going to cry and I couldn't bear it. She was my sister. My little sister. My heart just melted, Meena. I began to cry.

"Say it, Millie," she insisted. I kissed her then and said it. "I forgive you, Judith."

'All at once it was as if a burst of energy shot through her body. She laughed out loud and crushed me in a hug. Then she did something so out of character I didn't expect it. She tousled my hair with rough hands, pulled at my blouse so hard, it tore.'

'I saw my dad standing on the porch. And Mum too,' Millie sighed. 'And the neighbours, Rama and his wife—not Sundari, the first one she died of TB, did you know that? And that wild child Kitchibhai, he was there. He was everywhere, bloody nosey-parker, poking his nose into everything. I felt Judith grip my hand for a brief instant. Then in a flash, she was off, sprinting towards the house. She ran to my dad, and clutching his shirt, she spoke to him. As I came nearer, I caught the last bits of her words, urgent and loud enough for everyone to hear. God, was she earnest! "Don't be angry with her, Dad. Millie is just foolish and silly. I never knew about the salesman. Or I would have stopped it at once, or told you. This morning, when I found she was gone, I didn't stop to think. I just ran after her, I did. He was a useless bum.

Scoundrel. Look at what he did to me, I'm bruised everywhere—he pushed me to the ground, he did. But it's all right. The man's gone. And Millie's safe."'

Millie came closer till she was almost touching her sister. Judith gave her a quick glance before she turned her face away. She looked completely animated, even vibrant. The broken woman who had been weeping in Niles's veranda had disappeared. Judith spoke to their dad, 'I should have told you, I know. Should have woken you up this morning. I'm sorry, sorry, sorry, but we can still keep this quiet, Dad. For Millie's sake. For poor Millie.'

Millie paused to catch her breath. As she breathed, her breath rattled in her throat. 'For poor Millie, she said. For poor bloody stupid idiotic Millie. My dad shot me a look of pure astonishment. Judith gazed at me, deep with love. I gazed back at her. Then, for the first time in my life, with all the strength I had, I slapped my sister.'

Millie wept with the remembering. The tiffin carrier I'd brought lay on the table, forgotten, unopened. I went to her. After a while, I placed my hand on hers.

'What happened next?' I asked simply.

She blinked. Her eyes were on the photographs. 'It was the strangest thing. It got all hushed up somehow. I mean nobody really *believed* Judith. Then two years later, she married an English manager and they moved away to England. She got her English man after all. While I'm here, alone and alone and alone. Funny how things work out, isn't it?'

Millie refused to say another word. When I asked her to at least eat something, she shook her head. When I left her, she was lighting another cigarette, her eyes still on those photographs.

I walked back seething inside, sad and angry for Millie. When I reached Aunt Sundari's house, all the lights were switched on. Aunt Sundari was listening to a Tamil song request programme on the radio. She turned around and smiled at me. Without thinking, having entirely forgotten that I was supposed to be angry with my uncle and her, I ran and gave her a hug. It was a comfort having her arms around me. She was such an entirely normal, ordinary person.

'What's brought this on, Meena?' she smiled.

'Millie was telling me about her life. It's so unfair, Auntie,' I burst out. 'Judith manipulated people all her life and she got rewarded. Whereas, Millie—her life is gone and she is all alone. It's not fair, Auntie. Where's the justice?'

Aunt Sundari switched off the radio. She spoke so softly that I strained to hear. 'That poor thing. Is she doing it again? I must go see her now.'

'I don't understand,' I said.

'That's not Millie at Number Six, Meena. That's Judith. Millie married a Tamil school teacher and went to live in Bertram Estate. She visits once a year.'

END

3

Dey Raju

Tamil movies were mother's milk to me. When I was a baby, Amma used to smuggle me into cinemas giving me her breast to shut me up. Back then, cinema was the only entertainment apart from Friday nights at the temple. To miss even one Tamil movie was unthinkable. Amma wasn't going to have any of that—baby or no baby.

Inevitably, I grew up on a staple of Tamil songs, dances, actors and actresses. I knew all the lyrics, all the lines of great film scenes. My role models were the actors Shivaji and Gemini Ganesan; my sweethearts, Padmini and Savitri. I wanted my wife to look like one or the other, depending on which actress was the flavour of the month. Amma and Devika, my younger sister humoured me but Appa—Appa would merely snort and say, '*Dey* Raju, these romantic Tamil movies have become a life-support system for you. Utter nonsense.'

When I left home to work in Kuala Lumpur, I was mortified to discover that I was painfully tongue-tied before women. I turned beetroot and stammered pure gibberish in their company. All hopes of cutting a dashing romantic figure in their presence vanished almost on the first day. Romance therefore became fodder for lonely nights in my rented room. It took shape in the words I would speak to my future wife and the songs we would sing.

So, when Appa sent me a telegram, 'MARRIAGE ARRANGED. COME IMMEDIATELY' I was primed and ready. My mates at work ribbed me mercilessly about marrying a bride I had never seen but I was unfazed. Mine was traditional Indian culture with five thousand years of history. By golly, I was proud of it.

Travelling on the train, I had pleasurable thoughts about my future bride until an elderly neighbour from home, Auntie Rukku, came to sit across me. 'You mean you haven't set eyes on your bride? Don't even know her name?' She wheezed with laughter. '*Dey* Raju, for a young modern boy, you are quite something.'

'It's our tradition, Auntie Rukku,' I replied through stiff lips. 'It's the way we've always done things.' Horrors, did I sound prim?

She patted my knee cheerfully. 'Rubbish! That was in the old days, dear.' She turned dreamy. 'Even I had a good look at who I was marrying, long before the wedding. Of course, they check everything out, find out about family, character, habits, occupation, everything but still . . . I even talked to my future husband when they came to ask for my hand.' She smiled pityingly at me. 'I never thought, in this modern world—1965—I'd meet such a conservative young mind.'

I smiled politely. Inside, I was seething. Who asked these crones anyway? Still, the first feelings of unease stirred and they wouldn't go away.

Upon reaching home, I made for my mother. It appeared the whole neighbourhood was milling about in my house. Weddings were after all, a neighbourhood affair. Kitchibhai, the local thug and childhood friend, was directing his minions as they put up yet more lights in the doorway.

The house was a dazzle of wedding display. Crepe paper in all hues of the rainbow was draped around pillars, down the banisters and hung in loops on the ceiling. The ubiquitous banana trees stood sentinel at the front door while at the gate, a banner proclaimed 'Welcome' in all the Malaysian languages. Kolams, rice patterns, in the porch and just inside the house. Coconut fronds danced gently as they framed the entire front of the house. The record player blared away, playing wedding songs from films. I knew all of them by heart.

The whole scene was over the top. It was absolutely wonderful. It took some time to find Amma. She was not in the kitchen where women stirred curries and cleaned huge mounds of banana leaves on which to serve food. I didn't know I had so many relatives and neighbours. The professional cook, hired for the occasion, casually dropped pieces of vegetarian fritters into boiling oil. He had a cheroot in his mouth which he took out now and then to flick the ashes into the sink. Dressed in a once white dhoti, he looked bored. He could have done his job in his sleep. Amma wasn't in the bedroom either, where my aunts were arranging silk sarees, veshtis, fruits, betel leaves and sweets on trays.

I finally located her in the bathroom with Devika. Amma was dyeing her hair, chanting the familiar mantra. 'It's sooo unfair. I'm a good ten years younger than your father but does he have any white hair? Nooo. Not one, whereas . . . '

It was no matter that Appa was almost bald; the point being, what was left of his hair was shining black.

I had more urgent matters to think about. 'Amma! The bride! Tell me about her!'

Devika got in first. 'Oh, you struck the lottery, big brother. She's Appa's boss's daughter. Built like a battleship. They sold you for fifty pounds of jewellery and a house.'

I paled considerably. Fat was fine. My Savitri, past her prime bloomed to beyond 'generously endowed' but . . . battleship? Then again, Devika was such a disgraceful tease.

'Amma!' I gasped.

'It's a match made in heaven.' Devika was like a dog with a bone. 'Skinny brother and titanic sister-in-law.'

'Oh, shut up, girl,' Amma was cross. 'Go to the kitchen and do something useful.' Devika flounced off, her laughter ringing in my ear.

Flustered and only half-dyed, Amma babbled, 'Oh, don't disturb me, Raju. There's nothing wrong with your bride—I mean—it's such a little thing you'd hardly notice . . . go ask your father, he arranged everything.'

This was not good. Not good at all. You can't ask your father these things. Judicious bribing of Devika revealed the bride's party was staying at a neighbour's nearby. This was a relief as Appa's boss's house was two hours away by car.

I collected Kitchibhai to casually saunter over to the neighbour's house. 'You mean you haven't seen the bride? *Dey*, you are either very brave or totally mad!' Kitchibhai rubbed his hands with glee. Perhaps it was something recent in the air or water but I got the notion that the population in my hometown had become distinctly an unsympathetic lot.

Just like mine, the neighbour's house was bathed in the usual wedding paraphernalia. Indeed, it appeared louder, gaudier, brighter if that was possible. In the mass of people coming and going, we managed to get in the house without anyone being the wiser. The neighbour's giggly brother told us that the bride was in *that* room. We crept along to take a peek.

She noticed us at once. I mean it's hard to creep about unnoticed when your turban is flaming red. I pinched Kitchibhai. Surely, he could have worn a less noticeable headgear. She screamed and rushed out and screamed and hooted with laughter all at the same time. She *was* built like a war ship. Like a mountain. Her valiant pink saree stretched to breaking point. My Savitri was positively a waif next to her.

'Hello, the groom, are you? Looks like you can't wait! Just a few hours only-*lah* then you can see to your heart's content!' She simpered, shaking her head coyly.

I stood rooted to the ground. My insides shrivelled up. I swear I could feel them curling up to die. 'Shy, are we? Can't have that, you know. Turn around, let's have a look.'

I don't know where my voice came from. 'I'm not the groom. I'm here to warn you—don't marry that fellow. Completely unreliable and irresponsible. Smokes like a chimney, drinks like a fish and a girlfriend in every department in his office. His parents don't know. Bad mistake marrying him. Whole life will be ruined.'

I fled. Kitchibhai rolled along slowly after me, stopping every now and then to laugh out loud.

'*Dey*, Raju!' He called out. 'I'm getting front row seats for your wedding-*da*!'

That night, I begged my parents to call off the wedding. 'I can't marry her. I'll run away!'

* * *

Appa decided his word was more important than my 'romantic Tamil film nonsense'. He said he would spend the night in my room 'just in case'.

I became the prisoner of my family. As Appa lay on my bed, watchful and awake, I prepared to sleep in the balcony. I didn't care to share the same room with my jailer. A man's got his pride. Luckily the weather was sultry. I get chilblains when it gets cold.

Well, there we were, settled somewhat for the long sleepless when there was a flurry of footsteps in the room. Amma, Appa's boss and two other women. I recognized Pink Saree. She glared at me, wagging her finger angrily. I thoughtfully scurried behind Appa's bulk.

'Ramanatha,' Appa's boss spoke to the floor. 'There's a bit of bother. My daughter wants to speak to the groom. She won't go through with the wedding otherwise.' He shook his head. 'These young things—I mean . . . ' He didn't complete his sentence.

'I want to speak with him alone.' The voice was husky, aching with hurt. It didn't belong to Pink Saree. I turned towards it.

The instant I saw her, something peculiar happened in my heart. As if a thousand bits of happiness flooded in, lighting it up. An impossible gladness seized my chest spreading through my body.

She was neither Savitri nor Padmini; neither fat nor skinny. She was just—she was just beautiful and she was mine. Her eyebrows were delicate new moons and her nose, her mouth, chiselled like a Grecian statue. A lock of hair fell on her forehead and her hands were clutching, twisting the ends of her long plait.

My face stretched into an inane grin. I couldn't help it. I tried to lock her eyes with mine but she was staring intensely at a point just beyond my right ear. Slow on the uptake, I realized somewhat belatedly that her eyes were not just staring but flashing anger and scorn in my general direction.

'We can talk over there.' I gestured towards the balcony unsteadily. As she swept on ahead, I caught the heady whiff of jasmines in her hair. Her nose ring glimmered in the soft light of the stars. It was undoubtedly diamond. I drew the curtains to give us privacy. Pink Saree wailed, 'You can't speak to him alone!' and waddled in to join us.

'Out!' We both cried.

Alone with her, I forgot Pink Saree and the family on the other side of the curtains. I forgot too, every single line of the Tamil love scenes I'd so assiduously memorized for ever so long.

In the darkening night, my love turned to me, her face aflame with pain. Yet, she wouldn't look into my eyes but at the same point somewhere beyond my right ear. The pebble dropped and I understood.

'You are squint-eyed.'

She lifted her head. 'Why else do you think you're getting a house and all that gold jewellery? For my father's wealth, I could have married someone far richer or better educated.'

My beloved had talons.

'Ouch,' I grinned. 'Why didn't you have an operation?'

'When I was born, I brought my father tremendous business luck. He didn't want to ruin it. Does my . . . does it revolt you?'

'I think it's charming.' I wanted to hold her, touch her, run my hands through her hair.

'So. My cousin Bhuma said . . . '

Bhuma. Mother Earth. If my beloved could keep a straight face, so could I.

'Those things you said to my cousin—are they true?'

'Your cousin? I thought she was the bride. I was petrified. I had to say something, anything to stop the marriage. It's not that I have anything against large women, you understand—my Savitri . . . you know, the actress, isn't exactly known for her slender figure . . . ' I was babbling again.

'Hush!' She demanded. 'It was all lies, then?'

Suddenly, it mattered immensely that I was honest. I answered slowly. 'I do smoke and drink occasionally—my parents don't know about that—but no I don't have a girlfriend at all.'

She did not respond immediately. Then, 'Bhuma's married with a child,' she said inconsequentially.

We were silent for a moment when all at once her hand shot out and she pinched me in my midriff. 'You will never lie to me?'

'No.' My voice was firm. 'You will never have to sift through my words. I will always speak the truth and so will you.' She sighed then, a curious sound of relief and lightness.

I wasn't finished. 'And you will never pinch me like this or else—'

'Or else?' Her voice shook and she looked at me, her mouth open, half wondering, half mocking.

I swear I didn't plan it. Of its own accord, my hand moved to the back of her head. In one fluid movement it pulled her to me and I kissed her deep on her mouth. It was unbearably sweet.

She didn't draw away immediately. I think we were both a little shocked. Where had that come from? We broke apart. She raised her hand. I caught it and held it on my heart. It was pure instinct. There was no need for words. I felt soft with love. But there was one thing I had to know. 'Can you sing Tamil cinema songs?'

Her giggle turned into a snort. 'Tamil cinema songs? Stuff and nonsense.'

Even melting with love, I thought how much she sounded like my father.

END

4

My Mother Pattu

My mother Pattu graced our lives largely with her absence, for which my father and I, and to a lesser extent, grandma, were profoundly grateful. She descended upon us once a month to collect her allowance from grandma, loot the pantry, curse my father and cuff me on the ear. We breathed a collective sigh of relief when she went away, except for grandma, who wept in secret for the daughter she could not stand to live with.

When there was no Pattu, there was light. There was fun: cycling to the food stalls near the market with my mates for the best *kuay teow* in Mambang; playing badminton in the cemented patch in front of Ahmad's house; walking home with Rubiah after a party, together with the boys—Wong Seng Chye, Manoharan, Raju and Abdullah, who all fancied me like crazy; meeting up with the 'gang' in the porch in Mr Goh's house, talking, laughing, eating *kuaci* and drinking orange crush. It meant twice-weekly Carnatic singing classes with Auntie Sundari, a few doors away from home. Pattu tried unsuccessfully to stop my classes claiming they would give me ideas above my station for 'after all, you are going to marry a beggar'. Auntie Sundari's was one of the few houses in town to which Pattu was never invited.

When there was no Pattu, I could wear my bra from the shop instead of the tight fitting scratchy camisole tops grandma ran up on her sewing machine. They flattened my breasts and I hated them with a passion matched only by Pattu's insistence that I wore them.

There is a single framed black-and-white photograph of my parents in the cupboard in grandma's room. It was taken after their marriage in 1950. A Chinese man and an Indian woman in Indian wedding dress; my father looked like a bit player in a promotional shoot for some cheap movie where the budget did not run to hiring a real actor. With a slight build and delicately beautiful despite a ravaged expression, my father sat rigid, facing the camera. His already white hair was brushed back from his forehead, settling just above his shoulders. He wore thick gold studs in his ears, white shirt, white veshti, black leather shoes. He was not smiling. Pattu stood beside him, her sculpted features marred by the insolence in her eyes and a sneer tipping her lips. The heavy Kanjipuram silk saree that she wore could not hide the swelling of her belly. One hand rested on her hip. The other, more brazen, she placed on her husband's shoulder. Even the photo resonated with her energy, her restlessness. She looked all woman, not fourteen.

* * *

In 1965, twenty years after the Japanese Occupation ended in Malaysia, my father remained in thrall to the spectre of the past which haunted him as his constant companion, memory breathing into his sleep, where his body thrashed his bed, filling the room with screams and then whimpering cries for mercy. When this happened, grandma and I would rush to his room and grandma would apply sacred ash on his forehead and his chest. She said he was remembering the time he worked on the Siamese death railway during the war. At such times, he struggled between sleep and wakefulness, trapped in a hell-hole, unable to cross over to sanity, his body drenched with sweat, fat globs of water oozing from the pores of his soul as he begged the Japanese soldiers to kill him, once and for all, in the name of God. Till the day he died, he could not bear to look at a Japanese man, not even in a photograph in the newspapers.

When the war was over, my Indian grandpa found him wandering in the streets, a young half dead, skeletal thin Chinese man with a tortured face and grey-white hair, who refused to speak of his life before the war. Grandpa took him home and looked after him as if he were a baby. Except for a three-month strain, the men were devoted to each other until grandpa passed away eight years later.

Frail, yet with a cigarette constantly on his lips, my father safeguarded his Chinese identity as an entity separate from his life with grandma and me. He ate Chinese dinners cooked and delivered by Cheong Kee Restaurant in town. He wore striped pyjamas tailored by Nam Fook Tailors in Jalan Bandar. He listened to the Chinese channel on the radio, drank Chinese tea, read Chinese newspapers and the Straits Times and steadfastly refused to talk of anything from the time before he became my father. 'Why do you want to know what is no longer important?' he would ask, not looking at me. I was abjectly devoted to him, terrified of saying anything that could bring down the shutters on his face.

* * *

When I was ten, I asked Pattu if she loved me. 'Love you, Lalita?' She drawled. 'Stupid question. As stupid and ugly as you. I was fourteen when I had you—that big horrid thing that swelled my stomach, gave me heartburn and cost me my life.'

'Oh come now, Pattu, surely . . . ' Grandma's voice tapered off.

'She cost me my life, Amma,' Pattu insisted. 'Everything came to an end with you, idiot girl. And don't forget, ten hours of pain before you were born.'

'It was a very short labour. Even the doctor was surprised,' Grandma said.

'No, ten hours. So much pain. God, I was sick of you already.' Pattu boxed my ears and turned away.

I was shocked at first that a mother would not automatically love her baby but it was a secret relief to hear her words. I was free then to hate Pattu without guilt.

Pattu was the bile that I retched out after each of her visits. She was the screaming in my head whenever I could not answer her quickly enough, receiving a sharp slap as reward. She was the poison leaching my blood, my bones and that was the real nightmare, for if you discounted a few details like my hair, skin colour or eyes, I was a dead ringer for her. I could not bear the horror of it. There was nothing of my father in me, nothing, for he was not my father. Everyone knew that story. I knew it soon enough, in the way children absorb stories almost through osmosis, though Papa never spoke of it, nor did grandma.

I knew how Pattu silently pointed to Papa when her parents discovered she was pregnant. I knew how grandpa beat him with his fists, yelling the pain that rose from his stomach: 'I saved your life, you Chinese bastard, I saved your bloody life and you do this to me?' I know that Papa did not fight back. He merely repeated: 'I have never touched her.'

I heard how grandpa clutched my father's feet and wept when I was born: I had green eyes and hair the colour of wheat.

* * *

I never called her Amma. She was always Pattu right from the time she ran away with a travelling salesman, two weeks after the thirty-day lying-in after giving birth. But before running away, she helped herself to cash from grandpa's strongbox and several gold chains. Six months later, she returned, sans money or gold or salesman, a seething brittle creature who, the neighbours said, pinched me black and blue when she thought no one was looking. After that, it was a series of ding-dongs, run away with somebody or other, with whatever valuables she could lay her hands on, come back empty-handed, run away, come back again, each time quicker to anger, feverish discontent biting at her ankles until grandpa gave up and bought her a house ten miles from Mambang where she could live alone and do as she pleased.

There were no secrets to be had in our home, in our neighbourhood. Everything was out in the open—who drank on the sly (Auntie Judith, who wrapped her daily beer bottle in a newspaper and sneaked it home); who demanded money under the table for doing his job as a clerk in the government (Abdullah, Hassan and Chandran); who beat his wife (that list was too long) and who got himself a mistress (Ah Seng); who went to the bomoh for desperate spells to keep her straying husband (Fauziah, whose husband was eyeing a third wife); and who was Pattu's latest lover. There were no secrets, true, but none was paraded in the open. In public, we were deeply conservative and so staunchly upright you could balance a spoon on us. All except Pattu.

There's a story that has turned into local legend: when Pattu was at the market one day, she overheard a man-about-town making unfortunate remarks about her morals. Pattu tucked her saree into her waist, strode up to the man, grabbed his shirt, and thrashed him. 'Oh, how he tried to run, Lalita,' said Auntie Jansi, a neighbour, when she related the story to grandma and me. 'Like a whirling demon she was; she punched him and tore off his clothes and she stomped on him and described his manhood with choice profanities.' I looked bewildered. 'Bad words, girl,' she explained. 'Pattu is many things, but you know what? That day, when she beat up that miserable bugger, it was like all the wife-beaters and all the snarky men got a taste of their own medicine. My heart glowed.'

I must have scowled for she continued. 'Pattu . . . Pattu is just Pattu. She'll give us her last dollar without a thought . . . '

'Then she'll come home and give me a slap,' I said. 'But no more. Papa said . . . '

'Hush, Lalita,' Grandma stopped me, her eyes pleading.

'Even the beggars adore her. She's welcome everywhere except over there . . . ' Auntie Jansi flicked her head at the general direction of Auntie Sundari's house.

'Pattu is a generous woman,' Grandma agreed. 'She's good in the heart. She loves everyone. It's just her family she can't stand.'

'No, Grandma,' I said. 'It's just Papa and me she can't stand.'

Grandma sighed. 'She craves the things she can't get. But I won't let her hit you any more, Lalita. No, enough already. I mean it.'

'Why does she do it?' I asked. Grandma looked away.

'Think back to last Friday,' Aunt Jansi said.

We had been walking back from temple that evening, a group of us from the neighbourhood. Papa was away in Kuala Lumpur. The women were draped in sarees; I wore my silk pavadai. We wore flowers in our hair, bangles on our wrists. Grandma's gold jimikis glittered in my ears. In the temple, at least three boys kept looking at me when they were supposed to be praying. My cheeks flushed, my eyes shining, I felt high as a kite.

As we crossed the street from the temple, we saw Pattu talking to a man in the shadowed doorway of a shophouse. We could not see their faces clearly but Pattu was leaning against the doorway, her hand glancing light on his shoulder. I knew though I could not see, that she would have arched her eyebrows, a smile playing on her lips, laughter waiting impatient at her throat. After all, I knew my mother. I did not know the man though. There was a dignity about him, uncommon in most of Pattu's men friends.

'Let's take another route,' I said at the same time Grandma called out: 'Pattu!' Pattu turned and her eyes narrowed when she zeroed in on me. My heart dropped like a stone.

'Namaskaram,' the man greeted us. 'Who is the child?'

'My granddaughter, Lalita,' Grandma said, her voice uneasy, recognizing too late the expression in Pattu's eyes.

'Beautiful child,' he said, 'like the goddess Lalita herself.'

'What are you all waiting for? Go home.' Pattu's voice was a machete slicing me wide open, spilling blood. We straggled home in silence. Once inside the house, Grandma and I waited. I began to sob. 'Maybe she won't come, Lalita,' Grandma said. 'Maybe she has already gone back. It's late.'

She came, her hands fuelled with bitter rage. I did not make a sound. Grandma shrieked, 'Aiyoh, aiyoh, aiyoh!' tears falling down her cheeks. Afterwards, she tried to rub some ointment on my body but I pushed her away. 'You didn't stop her,' I railed. 'I wish she would die. Just die, you understand? Just die and leave us in peace.'

Papa's face was white when he saw the bruises. 'If you let her touch my daughter again, we will both leave this house and you will never see us.' Grandma wrung her hands and cried. For the first time in my life, I didn't believe a word Papa said. Didn't he know Pattu hit me every single time she visited? Did he think spending his days at work and his evenings in the Chinese Recreation Club gave him reason not to know?

* * *

A week later, *The Sound of Music* was finally playing in our town. The excitement among my friends—gosh, it was like a fever. We knew all the words to all the songs. We sang them during recess in school and in between classes. We were going to catch the afternoon matinee on Friday since school finished early. Rubiah had bought the tickets. I was to cycle to her house and then together we would go to Meena's where three other girls would be waiting. After the movie, it was to be *ice kacang* at Uncle Wong's stall in time-honoured tradition. Papa was in Kuala Lumpur again, this time for a medical appointment with a specialist. He would be away for five days but had already given me money for the cinema ticket plus a bit extra. My heart would not stop singing that day, I was that delirious.

I rushed home after school on Friday to change out of my uniform. Pattu was there. She was at the dining table, with our neighbours, Auntie Jansi and Auntie Leela, waited on by grandma who, I noticed, had made her daughter's favourite dishes. They had finished their lunch. Pattu took out a wad of cash from inside her blouse, peeled off a few notes and handed them to Auntie Leela. 'Here, Leela, buy something for yourself and for God's sake, hide the damn money from that drunken lout of yours.' Auntie Leela's face shone. Pattu smiled, looked up, saw me and her face changed. 'What are you looking at, sour face?' I had told myself I would never let Pattu beat me again but when I saw her, my insides shrank and my heart thudded so violently I thought they would be able to hear it. My hands shook so I had to hold my schoolbag tight to hide the trembling.

'Gr-grandma, I-I'm g-going to take my shower n-now.'

'Oh yes, child,' Grandma smiled. 'You're going to see the film today, right?' Too late, she clamped her mouth shut.

'What film?' Pattu wanted to know.

'Nothing, Pattu. I made a mistake,' Grandma said.

'What film, Amma?'

Auntie Jansi stepped in. 'It's an English movie, Pattu. *The Sound of Music*. Very famous movie. Every kid is singing the songs. Everybody wants to see the movie including me, my children and even my mother-in-law. That's all. It's nothing to get uptight about.' She looked at me. 'You go bathe, child.'

'Oh ho! Going to see an English film. Going to dress up nicely is it, this English missy, to go out with boys to watch an English film?' Pattu drawled. 'Go, child, go and bathe and get ready.' Pattu's mouth curved into a small smile even as her eyes turned hard and I knew then that she had known all along about me going to see the film.

'Grandma!' My throat choked.

'Go and get ready,' Grandma said. As I walked up the stairs, my legs felt like lead. I heard grandma cajoling. 'Please Pattu, the child has been talking of nothing else but this film for weeks. Don't ruin it for her.'

I bathed and wore my newest outfit. Papa had bought it in Kuala Lumpur—a thin, delicate peacock blue pleated skirt, daringly three inches above the knee and a white blouse with a lace collar. I looked in the mirror and saw my face, pale, puffed up. Eyes dulled. Perhaps I could hide in the room until Pattu left, I thought. I could still catch the movie another day. I looked in the mirror again and saw my face mutating into my grandma's. Even as I dithered, a strange sensation blazing white with cold ferocity swept over me.

'We'll see if she dares to go,' Pattu was saying softly as I came downstairs. 'When I'm done with that missy . . . '

'I am going.' There, I said it, though my voice wobbled a bit.

'Ho-ho, the worm turns!' Pattu looked me up and down. 'Look at the skirt, so short, you can see her arse. Why bother to wear it, huh?'

In a second, she was in front of me. Her hand grabbed my skirt. There was a ripping sound. She raised her hand again. My hands caught it in mid-air and I pushed her away. Her other hand swung up and yanked my hair hard.

I felt no pain, nothing but that white cold anger that coursed through my body. I sensed rather than saw, Auntie Jansi and Auntie Leela pulling a cursing, shrieking Pattu away and sticking her on a chair. 'Have you gone mad, Pattu?' Auntie Jansi. I sensed grandma wailing, 'Aiyoh, aiyoh, aiyoh', hitting her head with hands. I sensed it in slow motion like someone in a fog for my vision wasn't very clear all at once. I knew though, what I wanted to do. I took my father's walking stick and I stood above Pattu and I raised it high with both hands. I did not say a word but there were noises growling at my throat. Grandma flung herself at Pattu and shouted: 'No, Lalita!'

The stick remained in my hands. 'Don't become like her!' Grandma said.

The stick was stuck to my hands. I could not lower it. Pattu's voice in the background: 'She wants to hit me? I'll kill her.' And Auntie Jansi: 'Shut up, Pattu.'

'You're not Pattu, you understand? Lali?' Grandma said.

It took me some time before I threw the stick down. Grandma turned to Pattu. 'What is the matter with you? You want to kill your own daughter?'

'I'm not her daughter.' I said, rubbing my head. It throbbed with shooting pains.

'No, you're just a bloody whore who took away my life. You and your father.'

Grandma said, 'Pattu, not this again . . . '

'Whore, I say. Whore!' Pattu used *theyvadiye*, a Tamil word for whore that was unspeakable, a word that once uttered meant there was no going back for speaker and listener. Spittle sprayed from her lips as the women looked at her in horror. Grandma pressed her hand against Pattu's mouth.

'I'm not the whore here, Pattu.' My voice was level.

'Pattu, from the time you were twelve,' Grandma knelt before her daughter, her face wet. 'I could do nothing with you. No tears or threats or begging could shift the lies. Telling your father you were doing needlework with Judith when you were partying with her and the white sailors. I tried locking you in your room . . . '

' . . . but I just climbed out of the window.' Pattu rocked herself. 'It was a prison, Amma. Don't do this, don't do that. Don't go there. Don't talk to boys. Don't dress like that.'

'It's the Indian Handbook on Bringing up Girls, Pattu,' Auntie Jansi said. 'Every Indian family had it.'

'I just wanted some bloody fun, Jansi. What's wrong with that? Instead, I got the family honour constantly shoved down my throat. Couldn't breathe.' Pattu took a deep breath. 'Still can't,' she said as if to herself.

Grandma said, 'I hid everything from your father. He never knew. Not about the white sailors who plied you with chocolates or the times you slipped away from home to go to the cinema with some boy . . . '

'Don't talk to me about my father. That man stopped me from going to school. School, Jansi, can you believe it?'

Grandma was about to say something but Pattu waved at her to be quiet. 'The nuns actually came to my house and begged him to let me continue. Said I was the best student in the class—that I could amount to something. But he—'

'You had reached puberty, Pattu. Your father was old-fashioned,' Grandma said.

'I could have become a teacher, Amma! Or a police inspector! I could have become someone!'

Grandma hit her forehead with her palm. Auntie Leela made murmuring noises of sympathy.

Pattu shrugged. 'Those white men were a different world. You know what, if one of them had said, "Come away with me, girl" I'd have gone, without a thought. Like that.' She snapped her fingers.

I did not want to listen anymore. I felt wiped out, emptied, without any thought or sensation. Except, one small part of me kept going back to that young girl, a little younger than me, who tried to escape from her cage only to find it growing bigger and bigger. I walked up the stairs to my room to change my clothes.

Auntie Leela's voice floated over: 'Pattu, you are the most generous friend I have, but when you curse and beat Lalita, it's not right . . . '

There was silence. Then Pattu said, 'She's living the life I wanted.'

I paused on the stairs. Pattu said, 'I won't have it, I tell you. I won't let her.' There was silence for a bit and then she laughed. 'She'll marry a bloody beggar; I'll make sure of that. You just wait and see.'

I selected a bright green skirt, folding up the waist several times so that it was five inches above my knees. I cycled with my friends to the cinema to watch *The Sound of Music*. I could not remember a single scene from the movie.

END

5

Charan

Five days after Charan's death, Shiva Das took the remaining urn of his son's ashes to immerse them in the waterfall behind his parents' house in Mambang. It was the place of Charan's childhood, the place where he had been happiest.

This was the last goodbye after the send-off at the waters off Port Klang. From earth to fire to air to water, Charan's last remains, all that was left of him, became one with the elements. There was no need, though, for this last rite; everything that could be done to ensure peace for Charan's soul had already been performed.

'So why you want to do it?' Sulo asked that morning when Shiva Das announced what he planned to do. 'Big melodrama, izzit? Why suddenly, you're the great grieving father?'

Of late, the sharp bits of broken glass hidden beneath Sulo's words had come out into the open, glinting rage, impatient to hurt and hurt quickly.

When did it happen? He knew exactly to the day—six months before, when Charan came to stay with them for good, after his grandfather's death. The daily presence of her son triggered all the old humiliation turned guilt turned resentment turned fury turned violence. Strange, he thought, that he was able to analyse the situation without being able to do anything about it, whether for Charan's sake or his own.

The violence had escalated just ten days before, when for the first time in years, the whole family had come together for Sulo's birthday. Suresh had flown down from Boston and Uma from Sydney. Her engineering consultant son and orthodontist daughter—Sulo was beside herself with pride at the party. My children, my children, she kept saying until Charan asked: What about me, Amma? 'You are your father's son, no doubt about it, madaiyan,' she replied. 'All the brains are from my side of the family. I got a first grade in Form Five. Your father got only a third grade.'

'Brains are no good if they're mean, Amma,' he said, getting a knuckle knock. 'Madaiyan, madaiyan,' she muttered.

'Stop calling him stupid, Amma,' Uma's voice was sharp. She put her arm around Charan. 'You want to come back with me to Sydney, Charan? For a few weeks?'

He grinned at her. 'Only if you promise to sing me a poem, Akka.'

'I don't get it.'

'My Thatha was my first hero. Suresh Annan was my first buddy. You were my first song. Amma was my first bad dream.'

'And Appa? What was he?'

'I don't know.' He looked at Shiva Das and tried to figure it out. 'Nothing,' he shook his head. 'What are you, Appa?'

Nothing.

'So, why you can't throw his ashes here in the garden? Why you must go to Mambang?'

'Please Sulo, let's not argue over this, for God's sake.'

'Oh, oh, oh, oh. Yeah, I saw your martyr show at the funeral. Fantastic performance. The poor grief-stricken father carrying the pot around his son's coffin. Everybody felt so sorry for you. No father should have to do the funeral rites for their children and all that sodding stuff.'

'Amma, stop it!' Suresh said. 'What's happening here? Look, we're gonna sort this out right now. Sit, both of you.' He pointed to the dining table. Sulo placed herself next to him.

It's not right for the child to go before the parent, Shiva Das thought, as Uma linked her hand with his, as they sat at the table. How can it be? Your son lies in his coffin and you, the parent, carry an earthen pot of water on your shoulder and you go around his body three times and each time, the vettiyan, the graveyard caretaker, knocks a hole on the pot with a sickle. One knock on the pot, two, then a third. The water gushes out, mimicking life leaving the body. At the end when he had to smash the pot on the ground to release the soul from the prison of the body, he couldn't do it. It was the vettiyan who took the pot from him and threw it onto the ground. Strange how his mind remembered the minutest detail—the way the clay shards jumped and scattered and the water lay on the ground, a puddle seeping into the ground, disappearing into the earth even as he watched. Strangely, that gave him immeasurable comfort and he lit the pyre with a steady hand. Besides, in the cemetery, with the logs of wood covering the body, it was not Charan who lay there but a stranger.

Sulo could not wait to begin. 'I was a good mother. To all of you. Don't you remember? I put the alarm at five in the morning so I could fix a proper breakfast for you both . . . '

'Amma,' Suresh said. 'You were a wonderful mother to Uma and me.'

'That's right. Everybody said so, you know. They said, Sulochana is an amazing mother and that's why her Suresh and her Uma are so brilliant and they were top students in the school and they got scholarships to study overseas and now they're big and successful people. All because of their mother!'

'But Charan didn't fit the mould, right?' Uma looked at her mother. 'My baby brother was not clever, not quick—he was eighteen years old, going on ten. And he was always going to be ten. Amma, you resented him?'

'Of course not, don't look at me like that, Uma.' Sulo touched her daughter's face. 'I love all of you. Every mother loves her children. It was your father who hated him.' She glared at Shiva Das. 'He said . . . he said that boy was a blight on his life. He said it was not fair that he had to look after an idiot boy all his life. That he deserved a rest, now that his children were all grown up. He used to tell him to his face, you know, to go and die.

'Amma—'

'Let me finish, Uma. That day when you told Charan he was going to Sydney with you, your father went to him and yelled at him. Said, not enough ruining your mother's life, must ruin your sister's also. Yes, he said that. And he hit him—God, how many times, I don't know. Always knocking him on his head, calling him madaiyan, muttal, what not . . . '

'More lies? Your disconnect with reality, Sulo—'

'No, don't you *Sulo* me,' she cried. 'No use you using big words, disconnect or reconnect. I worked for this family; you didn't. Morning, maths teacher in school. Afternoon, night, math tuition. I worked day and night for this family. Twenty-eight years of my life. For my children, so they could become somebody big, you know.' She looked at her hands. 'And after all that, they still loved you best.' Her lips parted in a grimace. 'You—' she pointed at her husband. 'You did nothing. Just a clerk all your life,' she shrugged 'not your fault—wrong race, wrong religion, what to do, in this country—but you didn't fight, did you? No protest, nothing. You just came home every day after work to play badminton with the kids or kick a football or watch television.'

He spoke to her the only language she could understand. 'It's true. Everything Suresh and Uma have achieved, they achieved because of you, Sulo.'

Uma said. 'If not for you, I wouldn't be a dentist . . . '

'I wouldn't be an engineer . . . '

'Not dentist, orthodontist. And engineering consultant. Say it properly,' Sulo's voice preened.

Shiva Das laughed without mirth. 'Two brilliant children, then eleven years later came Charan, the dud. How you hated him. Poor Sulo—'

'Don't say that! No mother ever hates her child. It's unnatural. You hated him.' She turned to her children. 'He hated the boy. He hated him every single day. When the boy was three—'

'Charan! Charan, not "the boy". Call him by his name, Sulo. Say it!' Shiva Das reached out and seized his wife's hand. She shook it loose.

'I know his name, you don't have to tell me. You know, Suresh, when the boy was three, your father hit him and hit him again and again until he bled from his head . . . '

'I remember that,' cried Uma. 'Charan couldn't recite the alphabet—he'd say A, B, C and then he'd forget and start all over again—' Uma's voice was low as she searched her mother's face. 'You got madder and madder. You kept hitting him with a ladle. He was screaming and you wouldn't stop. We couldn't hold you away from him so Suresh threw himself on Charan and cradled him and I ran to the hall to telephone Thatha. I was crying, I remember. It was you, Amma, not Appa.'

They'd called their grandfather, not their father, thought Shiva Das. What would their father have done? Made feeble entreaties maybe. Cried and held Charan while Sulo beat them both? Even at that age, they knew their father.

'Thatha came and took Charan away,' Suresh said. 'Charan never lived with us after that, did he?'

'I don't remember any of that,' Sulo said.

'You called Charan stupid,' Uma shook her head. 'You've no idea how amazing he was. When we Skyped—'

'You Skyped with them?'

'Every two weeks, Amma. Once he told me, all his words were locked up in his throat. They couldn't come out. He said, "Uma Akka, can you get them out? Because you're a dentist."'

'Wait,' Suresh said. 'Remember, I told you this before, Uma. I was Facetiming with him and Thatha, and he said the neighbour had shouted at him. What did you do, I asked. And he grinned. "I told her, Mrs Ho, don't do a Sulochana on me. Been there, done that." And he gave me a high-five!' Suresh shook his head. 'From Mambang to Boston, my kid brother gave me a high-five! He wasn't a madaiyan, Amma. He was eloquent. You just never understood.'

Shiva Das found himself weeping inside. How did he not know his own children? How did he not know Charan? He had been so occupied feeling sorry for his son that he had failed to hear his voice.

'When I talked to Thatha,' Suresh's voice shook. 'He always said, "Look after your brother when I'm gone, Suresh." And I always said of course, Thatha, he's my brother. It's one of those things people say when they're not really taking things in.' Suresh buried his head in his hands.

'He told you that?' Shiva Das said to him. 'He told me the same thing.' He had said more. *Being a nice man is not enough, Shiva Das. Being good is not enough. You must be courageous as well. For God's sake, man, stop being a coward.*

'I'm sorry, Sulo,' he said, turning to his wife. 'I'm so sorry. I failed you. I failed my father. I failed Charan.'

'You're a total failure, I know, but I don't know what you're talking about now,' Sulo said. 'Listen, I didn't kill the boy. I didn't call him wasted space. I didn't give him your bottle of sleeping pills and tell him to take the whole lot.'

'What?' That was Uma and Suresh. Shiva Das closed his eyes.

'What, what?' Sulo demanded. She got up from her chair. 'I didn't do anything. Everything was your father's doing, understand? Anyway, he gave the bottle back, didn't he? He said—he said, "I can't do that, Amma. The knowing would eat your insides." Stupid boy. Talking nonsense.'

'And the very next day, he walked to the main road and stepped in front of a speeding lorry,' Shiva Das said.

He placed the urn carefully in a basket, holding it in place with his new veshti. He put the basket in the front passenger seat and strapped the seat belt across it.

'We'll get her proper psychiatric help, Appa,' said Suresh, giving him a hug. He nodded. 'Though I just don't understand how it could go on for so long without anyone doing anything about it.'

'Do you want me to come with you?' asked Uma.

'No, darling. I have to do this on my own.' He kissed his children and held them tight. It lay unspoken between them, a knowledge that he had disappointed them, a knowledge that no one was willing to articulate.

Mambang was barely an hour away. As he drove, Shiva Das thought about his father's words. *For God's sake, man, stop being a coward.* He *was* a coward. He knew that. Sulo frightened him. Confrontation frightened him. He was willing to put up with any number of indignities in return for the comforts of the familiar. He could have moved to Mambang and kept Charan safe with him. He didn't. Creature comforts were important. The familiar was comfortable. It hit him that while he had felt sorry for Charan, he had never valued him. Not once. He had never loved him enough. And so, Charan had paid the price. My God, he thought. Everyone I know is far braver than me. My father. My Uma, Suresh. Even Charan. 'Forgive me, Charan! I'm so sorry, son,' he cried out.

The Mambang waterfall. Charan loved it so much he could spend hours there. Shiva Das was there in no time at all. He stood on that isolated spot where sunlight dappled through the tree branches and danced on the water like a daily cliché on replay. He removed his shirt and pants; put on his white veshti from the basket and fixed it firmly around his waist. He felt a calmness descend upon him. So this was what it felt like—*shanti*—the peace that passeth all understanding. His papers were all in order. He had made sure they were, when he went to see his lawyer, the day after Charan's funeral. Everything would be fine.

Bare chested now, he took out the urn. Holding it gently with both hands, as if it were a sacred offering, he walked into the waters. His back was straight; his strides strong and sure-footed. As he walked deeper and deeper into the waterfall, as the water splashed on his head, he released the ashes into the water, his voice ringing out, calm and confident: *Om Shanti. Om Shanti. Om Shanti.*

They said later that he must have slipped on an underwater rock.

END

6

The Princess of Lumut

When we were children, my sister Leela and I failed our mother at every turn. It was not just that we were mediocre students—coming tenth in my class of forty was my best achievement ever while Leela was once placed fifth—but we were not even good at sports. 'What's so hard about running, I ask you?' my mother wanted to know. 'Putting one leg in front of the other as fast as you can, that's all, what. When Fauziah's mother shows off her medals and Ah Meng's mother tells me he's the first boy in class again, I don't know where to put my face.'

'Tell her Leela was once fifth in class,' I said.

'I did. Fauziah's mother said yes, yes but she was in standard 2E, wasn't she?' My mother felt the humiliation keenly because Fauziah and Ah Meng were my schoolmates and our immediate neighbours on either side of our house.

The area that we lived in was a potpourri in motion: children of all ages running in and out of each other's houses; where stray dogs lay in the shade of the Chinese and Hindu temple doorways at mid-day; where the women chatted with their neighbours in Malay, Chinese and Tamil. Wooden squatter houses with rusty tin roofs stretched right to the edge of the street. During thunderstorms, the rain hitting the tin roofs created a loud cacophony. Money was always scarce but almost every house boasted a neat garden of flowers, vegetables, and herbs on the outside, while large black and white photographs lined up just as neatly on the walls inside. One or two houses even had television sets which filled me and all the others who didn't have them with unbearable longing. It also meant that the entire street converged upon those houses on movie night. Seeing that Malay, Chinese and Indian movies were shown on different nights, that meant a minimum of three nights of neighbours packed into their tiny living rooms for those hapless households.

Ah Meng's mother sold vegetables in the market. Fauziah's mother worked in a factory while my mother cleaned houses, but aha—the crucial difference—my mother had a pension. My father, a labourer in the Public Works Department, died of a heart attack when I was one year old. My housewife mother, aged thirty, was pregnant with Leela. My father's boss, Tuan Haji Ali made sure my mother received the full pension. 'He was a god,' she said, of the boss, not my father. 'I should put a garland round his neck and worship him.'

'Leela and I could do some running,' I said, 'right after we wash the clothes and hang them out to dry and sweep the house and clean the yard and cook lunch and then mop the kitchen.'

'Or we could hit the books. After we wash the clothes and iron them and clean the house and weed the garden and cook lunch, mop the kitchen and run around the field,' Leela suggested.

'Dey!' my mother snarled. 'Other people get children who make their parents proud but I, I get clowns! What have I done to deserve this, hah?' She got up from her chair to chase us and what did she know, we could run!

I did not mind about Fauziah. I was in love with her. When I turned twelve and got hit by hormones, I wrote her a letter declaring my intentions. She responded immediately. 'Dey Krishna, you write me another rubbish love letter, I'll tell your mother and she'll whack you with her slipper. You just wait.'

Ah Meng, called Bones because he was plump, was another matter entirely, as he was constantly hanging about our house particularly during lunch and dinner. 'Bones, please,' I told him. 'You're not eating lunch at my house, okay?'

'You tell that to my stomach,' he said, calmly helping himself to rice and sambar.

'Will you still be eating our food when we're grown up?'

'Of course. I'm going to marry Leela and she'll cook for me.'

'Eeek,' Leela cried. 'Who wants to marry a fatso like you?'

Ah Meng was unruffled. 'Confucius says, "Love thy neighbour as thyself."'

'Dey, that was Jesus Christ, da.'

We did not know we were happy.

* * *

My mother stood at the door of my study, fidgeting, leaning on one leg and then the other until I noticed her. She was dressed in a sarong and loose cotton blouse, her hair grey-white, wispy, coming undone from its bun. From habit, I checked to see if the silver identification band was intact on her wrist. She was wily; she often managed to pull it off.

'Big brother, it's time for a story,' she said.

'Oh my God, is it time already?' I gasped and made a big show of dismay. Nodding yes, she squealed as I scooped her up in my arms and carried her to her bedroom. My mother was a tiny brown sparrow and weighed as much. At that moment, she was five years old. When we settled down to the story, she was always sixteen. Now and then, the sixty-two-year-old mother I knew peeked out, trying to make sense of the morass she was submerged in. Whatever her age, the bedtime story, the same bedtime story that she created and which I told, was a ritual written in stone that began when she stopped being the mother I knew a year ago.

Be grateful she isn't aggressive or violent, the doctor said. My mother retreated slowly at first and then with alarming rapidity into a younger self, always smiling, always gentle, but increasingly not present in the moment. When she was five, she was precocious. When sixteen, she was shy, blushing, a beautiful girl-woman standing on the threshold of love. Once or twice though, she managed to wander off and thus the identification bracelet on her wrist.

Sitting up in bed, she indicated where I was to sit—in a chair facing her. Photographs and framed newspaper cuttings covered the walls. They were all of me raising to the sky some medal or trophy I had won in badminton matches in my career as a champion. How assiduously she had collected the memorabilia over the years while I had chucked the actual physical mementos in some box where they were collecting dust. Or maybe I had thrown them out in the garbage. I cannot remember. I am not particularly proud of myself in those glory days. I play a better game now.

My mother waved a regal hand to all the pictures as if to say hello. Then she settled me with an eye and said, 'Story.'

I clasped my hands and began: 'Once upon a time, there was a beautiful girl who lived with her little brother and sister in a rickety old house in Lumut. They were very poor. They had no parents and sometimes they had very little food to eat and went to bed, still hungry. When this happened, they told each other stories to drown out the sounds of their growling stomachs. The girl cleaned homes and made sure the boy and his little sister went to school.'

'You forgot to mention their names . . . '

'Oh yes, the beautiful girl was called—'

'Rajam and the boy was called Krishna and the little girl was Leela.'

'Hey, who's telling this story, you or I?'

'You.' She giggled.

'Right. Just so we know. Now, where was I? Oh yes, the girl's name was Rajam but she was so beautiful that everyone called her—'

'The Princess of Lumut,' my mother breathed.

Leela entered the room at that moment. 'Does anyone want a hot Milo?'

'Shhh! Go away. My brother is telling a story.'

'He's not your brother, he's your son.'

My mother laughed, covering her face. 'Silly girl. I'm not even married!' She turned to me and whispered, 'That lady there, she's quite nice but so *sombong* and bossy!'

The Princess of Lumut had dark eyes, luminous like the moon. Her lips were rose-red. Her hair, lustrous and curly, fell to her hips. She was the most beautiful woman in Lumut town. Many men, all of them rich and powerful, wanted to marry her. They promised her all the food she could eat, all the money she could spend. They promised to look after her brother and sister. They promised her everything but she turned them all down. She had eyes only for one man, Chan Siew Kit, a great handsome prince. Chan Siew Kit was a noble prince, a brave and strong man who loved her and she loved him. They could spend hours talking to each other and when he kissed her, her heart floated right up to the stars. Chan Siew Kit finally asked her to marry him and go away with him to another country, Kuala Lumpur. She said no and turned him down and wouldn't tell him why. He tried to persuade her again and again but she always said, 'No.' Heartbroken, Chan Siew Kit left the town and went away forever. No one knew where he had gone. Rajam never explained to anyone why she had turned him down. She never married. She looked after her brother and sister and all her life, she remained a sad, lonely ice maiden. Sometimes, when she was too sad, she looked at the stars and asked them if they would take away her heart, please, so she wouldn't hurt so much.

My mother was falling asleep. 'He was a god,' she murmured. 'How can you marry a god? What would people say?'

Even when she was young, my mother could never have been described as a beauty. A timid bird of a woman, yes; with permanent worry lines on her forehead, stringy hair, plaited and rolled into a bun, a skinny frame and small breasts, whose dress was always a faded sarong and a cotton blouse. When we finally got Astro satellite TV, her highlight of the day was watching Indian serials on television after dinner.

Growing up, I had known nothing of the dreams that my Amma had woven in secret. The culture that bound my mother to lifelong widowhood at thirty could not fetter her desires. It snatched away her bright sarees, the flowers in her hair, the red pottu on her forehead. It dressed her in white and banished forever any remarriage, any sexual intimacy. Still, it could not prise away her longings that seeped out of locked cages in her mind. She was bloody thirty, pregnant, when her married life ended. Every night as we told the story, I felt knives stabbing, piercing my heart, tearing it to shreds.

Leela was waiting in the kitchen when I came out of my mother's room. 'I'm planning to go away this weekend to Penang,' she said, not looking at me. 'Meng has managed to get a locum so we can have the weekend to ourselves. No worries about the hospital calling him every few minutes.'

'Great. Enjoy yourselves.'

'You mean that?' She gave me a wary look.

'Is this the cue for me to play the heavy Indian brother protecting his sister's morals?'

'No! Don't you start!'

'Tell Meng I said hi. You going to make sambar for him by any chance?'

'Idiot!' She gave a shaky laugh. I held her close. Meng's mother had wept and begged and threatened suicide over the growing relationship between Leela and her son. It was the usual thing: she loved Leela, sure; but Leela wasn't daughter-in-law material because she was Indian. Meng's mother wanted a nice Chinese girl instead. She held out until she finally understood there would be no other woman in her son's life but Leela. My mother on the other hand, did not recognize her own daughter most of the time.

'I thought of driving down to Lumut,' I said. 'Nice drive, just over an hour. Amma would love it and we could drop by to see Mr Chan. I've got some micro-fine turmeric capsules from Germany. Guaranteed to reduce joint pain.'

She touched my cheek. 'You can't fight everybody's battles, Krishna.'

'Yes, I can.'

* * *

When Leela was born, my father was already a framed photograph on the wall. When Leela was six months old, my mother bundled her in a sarong which she tied to her back. I held on to her hand and together, we went from house to house, my mother cleaning them while I kept a watchful eye on the baby and kept out of everyone's way.

As we grew older, we took turns to help her with her work. Weekends and festivals were her busiest. One weekend, when I was thirteen, Leela was ill, so I went with my mother to a house I had not been to before. A bachelor's house, my mother said, very kind man, very neat.

I had just begun to sweep the porch when a voice called out, 'Hey, Thalaiva! What are you doing here?'

'Mr Chan Siew Kit Sir!' I stood to attention. 'I'm here with my mother, Sir! She's cleaning inside the house, Sir!' Mr Chan was the sports master, discipline teacher and school police chief, all rolled into one. I already had one run-in with him when I skipped badminton practice.

My mother rushed outside. 'Mr Chan, is my son disturbing you?'

'Hello, Rajam, this Thalaiva is my student in school.'

'Thalaiva? Oh no sir. Thalaiva means big boss. This one here's a useless student, Mr Chan, never studying, always failing his tests.'

'Trust my mother to staunchly support her son, Sir!' I said and held my breath.

He looked me up and down. He had his car keys in his hands. I wondered if he was about to gouge my eyes out. 'All right, wise guy, I'm already late for my badminton clinic in school. You come with me. Rajam, this useless Thalaiva is good in badminton but lazy. Never practises.'

My mother looked worried. 'He can't go with you, Mr Chan. He doesn't have a racquet.'

'I'll get him one.'

So began my new life under Mr Chan's relentless eyes, first as a school player and in a short time, as district and state player. *The racquet is not a thing apart, Krishna*, Mr Chan said, *it is part of you, an extension of your body. And you are not you, you are a warrior, facing a worthy opponent. Respect him but fight with passion, with every ounce of will power and intelligence within you.*

I did not play badminton. I waged war. The racquet became my weapon, the court, my battleground. Serve, smash. Take that, Puan Kalimah, Standard Four teacher, who used a ruler to part Leela's hair, checking for lice. She didn't check any other girl's hair for lice, for there was no other Indian in class. Serve, drop, feint. I battled Mrs Tan who called my mother *thangachi* with an exaggerated dance of the head. Mocking bitch. Smash. Smash. Smash. I battled the spectators who yelled, *Eh, Keling, balik India!* My racquet answered them: *No, I won't 'go back' to India, dickheads. I've never even been there. I'm as Malaysian as you are, get it?* I smashed Fauziah's uncle who forced her to stop running when he discovered religion. I smashed snooty Mrs Bala who accused my mother of stealing her gold chain and refused to apologize even after it was discovered exactly where she had left it. *Why should I apologize to my servant,* she asked.

As I grew older and more popular, I made deadly hits in shame at my mother's lack of ready money, at having to always depend on Mr Chan to pay for racquets and uniforms. I smashed in shame when I did nothing, nothing, but cringe when Mandy Wong laughed, seeing a faded middle-aged woman in an old sarong and blouse, seating herself in the stands to watch me play. I was madly in love with Mandy Wong of Upper Six and fantasized about her every night. I never told her that the *funny looking Indian woman* was my mother. Smash after vicious smash. Ashamed of my mother for not being beautiful—smash. Dreading the fact that she attended every single match—smash. *Take that, you stupid useless son for feeling ashamed of your mother. Take that, you bastards who call us keling and kling kwee, drunken blacks and pariah. Smash. Take that, you bigots who made Fauziah cry for being best friends with Indians and Chinese. Take that, you powers-that-be who refused to give me a scholarship. I got good enough grades to do engineering in university, didn't I? I was a state badminton player. I won any number of gold medals and trophies and I was from a poor home. You gave scholarships to undeserving jokers, why couldn't you give me at least a study loan? Because my skin colour was all wrong, right? Take that, and that, and that.*

* * *

My mother insisted on wearing a saree for the trip. 'I can't go to Lumut wearing a sarong, silly,' she said. We were prepared. It was a familiar argument. Leela had got a few ready-made sarees specially tailored for her. No widow's weeds for my mother. The sarees were deep red, mango green, sky blue. She picked the red saree with a gold border. Leela pinned flowers on her hair, fixed a pottu on her forehead and added a touch of lipstick to her lips. As Leela adjusted her saree, my mother giggled. 'I feel like a bride, Missy.'

'Don't call me Missy. I'm your daughter, Leela.'

My mother shook her head. 'You're a strange one, Missy.' She turned to me. 'I wish we could visit Mr Chan Siew Kit but he's gone somewhere.'

'We *are* going to visit him.'

'Really? The last time we went, there was an old man living in the house. He kept calling me 'Rajam' and I was angry. I didn't know him; how did he know my name?'

My mother sat at the back of the car. As I drove, she was in turns a kid, then a young girl and once, when she caught sight of herself in the rear mirror, she got hysterical. 'That bloody old woman can't leave me alone,' she screamed. 'Why must you follow me, old woman? Go away!' I stopped the car. It took some time to calm her down as she kept repeating over and over: 'She's evil, evil, evil, big brother. She follows me everywhere. Look, she's even wearing the same saree, the same flowers. Make her go away!' I made her sit where she could not see herself. Later, I saw her through the rear mirror, her face buried in her hands, shoulders shaking.

I didn't play competitive badminton anymore. I was too old, lacked the necessary agility but I still waged a mean war. I attacked the treachery of my mother's brain. *Take that, you miserable scum.* I hit it with all the natural remedies, prescriptions, brain activities and exercises I could find. My mother never understood why Mr Alzheimer was my deadly foe. *I can hardly roll his name in my mouth, big brother.* I hit deadly smashes into the rheumatoid arthritis that sneaked into Mr Chan Siew Kit's fingers and joints, swelling them and making it hard for him to hold anything, forcing him to hobble, forcing him to give up all games, this most decent human being.

When we reached his house, he must have heard the car for he came out, walking carefully with a cane. 'Mr Chan Siew Kit Sir!' I spoke. My mother turned to me, her eyes clouded. 'That old man . . . ?'

'Old man?' I said. 'Look carefully, Amma. Can't you see Mr Chan?'

'Mr Chan?' My mother was doubtful. She looked him, her eyes squinched. She stood unmoving, unblinking, her eyes focusing not on the man before her but on a memory scratching at the back of her mind. Then her face lighting up with a shy smile, she whispered, 'Chan Siew Kit. Chan Siew Kit!' Beaming, she went to him, and took his hand in hers.

'Hello, Rajam,' he smiled at my mother. Then, turning to me, he put his hand around my shoulders and said, 'Hey, Thalaiva. How have you been, son?'

I grinned. 'Still waging war, Mr Chan,' I said.

END

7

Invisible

Let me state upfront exactly what happened. I was washing the boss's car as usual at six in the morning. The sun wouldn't rise for a bit yet, but there was some light and the streetlights were on. A man approached me. He was a migrant worker like me. I knew that at once. Not an Indonesian, though. He smiled tentatively. I smiled back, my face plainly glad with welcome. That startled him somewhat. He came closer and offered his hand. I shook it and we chatted in Malay. That was the beginning. Within three days, I was embracing him, feeling his strength, running my hands over his hard body. We had merely minutes of privacy before the street awoke and people came out of their homes. Every second counted. I felt an excitement welling up in my body each time I saw him as if my own body had just awakened from a deep stupor and was ravenous.

We met in the mornings and again in the late evenings, when I took the dog for a walk. Snatched conversation, frantic groping. Happiness, happiness, happiness filling me up.

His stubble grazed my neck as he murmured, 'I want more, Ina, I want more.' So, it was. Twice. We were very careful, though. I had the house to myself when everyone left for work and school. Nevertheless, Indonesian and Filipino maid eyes were everywhere in the houses around. Linkhouses make it hard to keep secrets for long.

I made him creep around to the back, letting him in furtively. Then we scrambled to my room. For too long, it had been a tomb, mute characterless bit of space. Now, it was my bedroom. My bed came alive; I came alive.

Fulfilment. Tender loving spreading through my body. Such happiness that I just had to tell someone. I told Ohan, the Indonesian maid next door, stopping short of admitting I'd let him into the house. Saucer-eyed, she prodded me to tell her more but I kept from blurting out everything.

Perhaps to score brownie points with her own mistress, Ohan told her employer who then told mine. Mem, she got up extra early the following morning and from behind her curtains, watched as me and my man, we kissed and embraced and felt each other.

My Mem says I am not a bad woman, just someone they can trust no longer. Therefore, they are sending me back this afternoon, on a flight to Jakarta. From there I take a bus to my village, four hours on a rickety bus to return to my husband and two children whom I have not laid eyes on in three years.

Mem sprang the news of my return last night, at the last possible minute for fear I would run away. I surely would have. For good measure, she took the house keys up with her when she went up to bed.

My Mem, she says, 'You understand, Ina, I have children. I have to think about them. All the time, I used to feel safe because you were here when they came home from school. But now, you have a boyfriend. Sooner or later, he will want to visit you in the house. Imagine my daughter Uma coming home from school to see a stranger with the maid. Ina, she's ten. What if she gets attacked or worse, raped? What if Sunil, my baby, returns from kindergarten and you decide to run away and take him along? I can't take the risk, Ina. You have to go.'

My Mem is not paranoid. She is merely retelling horror stories that have happened again and again: *Indonesian maid kidnaps baby. Parents in a frenzy!* (Baby's, I mean).

Indonesian maid invites friend home who then rapes the child/ steals the jewels/Hi Fi system, TV, etc.

Police searching for Indonesian maid and her boyfriend who have trashed employer's house and disappeared, carrying with them undisclosed amounts of money and jewellery.

I understand her feelings perfectly. After all, I hardly know Ali except that he loves me—for now. Is he to be trusted? Is he the sort to steal or rape? I don't know. We are migrant workers, come to Malaysia in search of elusive wealth to feed and enrich our families back home. We come with our dreams shining in our eyes. The drudgery of our reality doesn't dim the facts: Malaysia is a paradise and the money we earn more than sustains our families.

Ali is an illegal, staying with a colony of other Bangladeshis in a shanty immigrant village in a patch of secondary jungle off Kuala Lumpur. It is deep enough to be safe from prying eyes; near enough to catch the bus to construction sites where the men work.

I am luckier than most other Indonesian maids. My employers whom I call Tuan and Mem, master and mistress, are decent folk. I watch TV soaps when the kids are in school. They don't stinge on food except there's no beef in the house. They are Hindus. Mem took me to a stall once and said, 'They have beef dishes here. Eat as much as you like—but you can't pack it home. We won't have beef in the house.' Funny, I've lost the taste for beef since.

During Ramadan, when we Muslims are required to fast from dawn to dusk, Mem said, 'If you are fasting, Ina, I'll get desserts for you from the Ramadan Bazaar on my way home from work.'

I gave a little laugh. I always laugh when I am sad. I thought of our meals back home. Rice, vegetables from the garden and a bit of salted fish. When the vegetables and fish ran out, we had hot rice and green chillies. When the chillies ran out, we had hot rice with a bit of salt. And when the rice ran out . . .

I smiled, 'I'm not going to fast, Mem. I've had a lifetime of fasting.'

Mem is modern. She wears business suits to work. She has no time for nonsense, no time for most things, really, for her office usurps her time and mind. When she's away from it for any length of time, her feet start tapping. She moves in jerky, swift steps and her speech—the words spill out before the mouth has time to form them.

She put her foot down when I first wanted to send my whole salary packet home. 'No, Ina, you must keep some money for yourself. It will be your insurance.' She opened an account in her name since I was not eligible, not being a citizen, and let me keep the bank book. It has grown to quite a bit. Today, she withdrew it all and gave it to me with a hefty addition from her husband and her.

My bags are packed. Riding on a wave of guilt, Mem has bought shirts, blouses, sarongs and T-shirts, clothes for my whole family, plus packets of biscuits and chocolates. There is no need for her to feel guilty at all. The guilt should be all mine, except I feel none, nor shame.

The first week here, surrounded by everything unfamiliar and frightening, I thought I would pine away and die. Sunil and Uma took me for a walk and we met all the other Indonesian maids in our area. They emerged like grey shadows from their houses, an unspoken signal informing each there was a new Indonesian in the neighbourhood. We chattered briefly and swiftly before they retreated back into their cocoons. I learned their names and which district in Indonesia they came from. They gave me their telephone numbers on tiny pieces of paper slyly hidden in the palm of the hand. Calls were safe to make when everyone, employer and child, was out. Even I knew that. I cannot tell how reassuring it was to speak in my own dialect with Marni who lived two doors down.

During festivals like Hari Raya Puasa and Hari Raya Haji, we Indonesians usually got the day off. We grouped together and the experienced ones knew exactly where to go. We made for Indonesian colonies and the satisfaction that came of being surrounded by my own people, talking of things we knew in the tongue I was born with was immeasurable. Potential husbands strutted their stuff among us, trying to pick us up while we shamelessly flirted and teased and yes, strutted about too. No matter that many among us were married and had children back home. That was another country, too remote and distant to affect the need for feverish contact among our own kind here. Our time was clouded with urgency for all too soon, we'd have to return to our daily identities as maids. Niceties, courting, we couldn't wait.

Mem let me call home once a month. There is only one telephone in my village in the wholesale dealer's shop. I call and hang up to call again in 30 minutes. In the meantime, a boy from the shop cycles to my house to let the family know. They pile onto bicycles or simply run all the way to the shop. In the meantime, I wait on a million tenterhooks for the sound of my husband, my daughter, Wati and my son, Yanto.

When it did go awry? Not at first. Not when I listened with proud tears in my throat as my husband said they'd repaired the roof, bought a pair of pants for Yanto, new sarong for my mother. Not when my Yanto said he was going to learn English so he could speak to Sunil. Not when my husband said they might buy a piece of land to build a better house. My heart felt like it would burst with pride—my money had wrought this change. *I* had wrought this change.

Towards the end of my two-year contract with the family, Mem asked me to stay on. It didn't seem like such a bad idea. I wanted to go back for a brief holiday but my husband persuaded me not to. It's only another two years, he said, then, you'll be back for good. If you come home now, you'll miss out on two months' salary, love. Why didn't I insist on going back?

Perhaps because I'd always been conditioned to obey. The subtle shifts in our relationship swept over my head, unrecognized, unheeded.

One evening, after Yanto and my Mum and my husband had spoken to me, Wati came on the line. Wati danced around a bit, talking about this and that, skirting questions about her studies. Then she announced baldly that she was getting married. Fifteen. When I was fifteen, I had her already but that was in those days.

'What about school? I thought you wanted to go to college.'

'No, school was boring,' she said.

'Can't you wait till I come back?'

'You're not coming back soon. I don't want to wait.' She cried a bit but there were threads of defiance in her tone. My baby. She seemed a stranger already.

'You can't wait for your own Mum, Wati? Your own mother? Are you pregnant?' I thought I sounded merely bitter and unbelieving. I wasn't aware of the whimper in my voice like a wounded dog. It rose to a wail and still I didn't hear it. Then my husband came on the line and asked for extra money for wedding expenses. It was only a wedding, he said. No matter. Nothing to get all worked up about. Why, when you come back for good, we'll have a big feast for her.

It became a norm after a while. After the pleasantries, came diffident requests for more and more money. As if my world over there was one open mouth that wouldn't stop feeding off me. It was leaching me bone dry and still it ate, voracious, consumed in its own feeding frenzy. There was nothing of me for myself. And so, I woke up one day, keenly aware that I too was hungry. For myself.

That's how I am now in the car with my Mem, driving to the airport. Mem is talking on the phone, promising she'd be on time for the meeting. I did manage last night to let Marni know to be sure to tell Ali. I saw him from my window this morning, standing bewildered by Tuan's car. Marni scuttled to him, spoke to him and scuttled back. I understood. She was going out on a limb for me and her employers—they weren't as nice as mine.

Sunil, Uma and I hugged when I was about to get into the car. Sunil cried and I kissed him. He had become my baby. 'Who will I tell my stories to when I come back from kindergarten?' he asked me, rubbing his nose on my blouse.

He'll tell his mum and dad. In the past twenty-four hours, they've moved closer to one another, as if the scent of my behaviour has united them, in the safety net of family.

In the side mirror, I see a motorcyclist speeding towards us. As the bike weaves through the traffic, I glimpse a familiar figure, sitting pillion. The bike draws alongside us and the figure waves at us. My heart turns over. Good old Ali.

I roll down the window and grin at him. The motorcycle drops behind us. I sniff the air.

'What are you doing?'

I turn to Mem with a smile. 'Breathing in freedom, Mem. Independence.'

'Oh, for heaven's sake, girl, don't make a drama of it.' Mem is brusque. She rolls her eyes. 'You're going back to your family—to your husband, kids—not to a prison, not to some ungodly end-of-nowhere place.' Her fingers grip and strain the steering wheel. 'I mean, you're not just a workhorse, you're the mother, the wife.'

I remain silent.

She turns to me angrily. 'Well, aren't you?'

I give a little laugh. Mem is working herself up, I can see.

'OK, your daughter got married without waiting for you to come home—Oh God, just fifteen, why the rush? They asked you for money for the wedding expenses, I know that was a bit too much . . . '

They asked me for money to buy the man a motorcycle so he'd be able to do business. They asked money to buy a mobile phone for my husband. He's also seen the most magnificent fighting cocks going for a song, can you imagine? They asked for more money because everything's now just expensive like anything and besides 'your sister and her two children are staying with us, apart from your Mum.' Oh yes, my twice-divorced younger sister. She begged to stay with my family while she put her life in order. My just-reel-them-in little sister.

'They're puffed up with my money, Mem. Not with love of me.'

'Not entirely true, Ina. They love you too,' she thought for a while and then added, 'surely.' For a few minutes we drive in silence. Then, 'Marriage is overrated,' she says, angrily honking at a car trying to overtake ours.

'Your marriage is sound, Mem, don't knock it. You have a good man.'

Her husband is amiable, a creature of comfort, just like mine. Give him his beer and his snacks and the sofa in front of the TV and it is enough. Now and then the children fling themselves on him and after the shrieks and protests and laughter, Sunil and Uma are on his lap, his arms around them, secure and content. 'He is . . . ' I think of a word to describe him. 'He's . . . solid.'

Her smile is brittle. 'How do you know?'

'I've seen the way he gazes at you when you're not looking. Besides, he's never made a pass at me.'

She laughs outright but we both know what I meant. Male bosses with wandering hands; bosses with more than wandering hands—why, we maids could write a book on them. Though to tell the truth, the culpability is often on both sides.

'He wants me to stay at home with the children,' she slips it in casually. 'Says he earns enough for all of us. Strange, as if one works simply for the money.' She doesn't wait for a response.

'I mean, I've been working for seventeen years. In my office, I'm not somebody's wife or mother. I am myself. I have my own identity. I earn my own respect. I am happy. It should count for something.'

I open my mouth to speak but already she's speaking again. 'It's not that I don't love my family. It's just that family doesn't fill me up enough. I want more. I want my own world, apart and separate from my home.'

Men can never understand that, not in a million years. Neither can many women. 'We've been born conditioned, Mem. See, a little leeway is okay as long as it is for the family. If it is for us, ourselves because we want more, goodness, that's selfish. We are women; we must submit, give in, compromise for the greater good of the family,' I intone loudly, raising a clenched fist to punch the air in the car. 'It is our role as virtuous women, our purpose in life, our responsibility!'

Mem looks at me in surprise. She bursts out laughing. I join her. Our laughter is uncontrollable. Mem has to park the car by the side of the road for a minute. She rests her arms on the steering wheel and laughs and laughs. Her voice shakes but she doesn't cry. It is I who cry. When she is more composed, we set off.

'It's strange isn't it, this conversation we're having, I mean we never talked like this when you were in the house with us.'

'But naturally,' I say. I am surprised at the question. 'Then, I worked for you. You were my boss and I was only the maid.' We'd shared the same house but had led entirely disparate lives. For when the work was all done and the parents were home, the children clung to them and I became an outsider on the fringe. They were together in a tight, cosy family circle while I became for the moment, a mere appendage. I didn't belong. Worse, I became invisible.

We are nearing the airport. I imagine my Ali will soon catch up with us.

'Why, Ina?'

I know what she means. 'Loneliness, Mem . . . despair . . . like a black hole sucking me in.' She shakes her head. I try to put it in words she can understand. 'I wanted more . . . '

I wanted to be visible. I wanted to be seen as me, Ina. Woman. Desirable woman. I wanted strong caring arms around me that craved *me*. Fidelity is only good when your man aches impatiently for you; when he wants you and only you. Fidelity. Ha! I think it was invented by men for women and only for women.

We park in the parking lot at the airport. Mem gets a trolley and we load my two bags on it. My handbag, I clutch it tightly. It contains all my money. Mem has my passport and the air tickets.

Somewhere here is Ali. Perhaps he is already in the departure hall, scanning the faces to reach me. The check-in counter isn't open yet. Mem taps her feet—the meeting is at the top of her mind and it is a long way back to KL especially if there's a jam and there's always one. Perhaps too, she's already regretting being rather open with me.

I look around. People, mostly Indonesians, mill about, pushing trolleys laden with bags way beyond the 20 kg allowed. Their chatter peaks and ebbs noisily; they are excited; sparrows comparing notes, exchanging numbers, addresses. The women are dressed to the nines. At any time, the counter will open and the horde will try some semblance at queuing up. There is hope in their shining eyes. Mine has not completely died yet. 'Mem,' I turn to my employer. My voice is soft with pleading. 'Please—what am I going back for?'

She doesn't want to look at me. She looks down at her shoes, high-heeled leather, very expensive. Immensely comfortable too, for I have tried on all her shoes.

'Please, woman to woman, what am I going back to?'

She looks up unwillingly. 'I'll get into a hell of a trouble with everybody, you know. Immigration, my husband . . . we may not be able to get another maid so easily . . . '

I grasp my chance. 'Please, Mem, just let me go to the toilet, alone. That's all I ask. Before the counter opens.'

She smiles. It's not a sad smile, nor a happy one. 'It's all right. I'll go to the toilet. Here, you hold the tickets and your passport. Stay here. I'll be right back.' She takes a few steps away and then comes back almost immediately. 'You realize you can never come back to our house?'

I nod.

'You will become an illegal. There'll be no safety. And where you're going, whatever you're going to do . . . it may lead you to only uncertainty.'

I nod again.

'This is a mistake, Ina. Don't do this.'

'Mem, what am I doing?' My voice is a bit unsteady. 'I'm waiting right here. You're only going to the toilet for a few minutes. What can happen?'

She looks at me for a bit. She smiles. At that moment, I am stronger than her. I don't tell her I have the addresses of all the safe houses I can go to, all the Indonesian villages in which I can disappear, right here in Kuala Lumpur. All of us Indonesian maids have them, gathered over the years from our network of fellow countrymen. She turns around and strides away, back straight, head stiff, steps long and jerky.

I stand still for a moment. I can see Ali in the near distance. He has seen me. Dear Ali. My heart surges with affection for him. Sooner or later, he'll surely tire of me or I tire of him. His loving kindness was enough for the time. He's probably married back in Bangladesh. If not, he'd want to return to marry there.

I think of the fresh-faced eager Ina who'd come to Malaysia to enable a better life for her family. She's long gone and I'm not sure I mourn her passing.

Ali's coming towards me, his movements impeded by the growing crowd in the hall. He waves, grinning madly. Quickly, I gather my bags. For a fleeting moment, my son's face flickers before my eyes. I push it firmly aside. All my life, I had been told what to do. Growing up a girl child, getting married, being a wife and mother, leaving home, coming to Malaysia, working as a maid; I had always listened and obeyed. The only thing I did all on my own was to choose Ali and make love to him. I liked it rather. It was heady, prescribing my own actions in my own life.

Ali is moving closer and closer towards me. So, bags in hand, I walk briskly in the opposite direction.

END

8

It's All Right, Auntie

Mum's run away again. I don't mean run away in the conventional sense. We went to visit her brother in Klang; when it was time to leave, she didn't. As usual. And now, Dad's not around. I woke up at half eight; he was gone. His car's missing. I'm all alone. I'm used to it though, not afraid or anything, just a bit hungry. I wish Mum would check to see if there's food in the house before she stays away. I mean there's a bit of bread but I can see some green furry bits through the plastic bag so I'm not even going to open it. I hope Dad buys something to eat when he returns from wherever he's gone, whatever time he comes back.

I clean my teeth and take a shower. I'm not allowed to boil water so I can't make a hot drink and my stomach's rumbling so I go open the front door, climb up the chain link fence and call out to Auntie next door. Her glass sliding panel has been pushed all the way back; only the metal grill is locked in place which means she can hear me.

'Auntie! I'm hungry. Can I have breakfast with you, please?'

Auntie bustles to her door as fast as her dodgy knee will let her. I climb over. Fierce-eyed, she's whispering to her husband. She's simply no good at speaking softly. Her voice carries and besides, I have sharp ears. She whispers in capital letters, 'NEVER CAME HOME AT ALL. THE MOMENT SHE GOES OFF,

HE TAKES OFF AND WHO CARES ABOUT THE KID?'
I pretend not to hear. It's better this way.

Auntie wears her hair bundled up at the back of her head with
a long clip but the frizz always escapes. Her hair's grey with streaks
of deep brown or burgundy or whatever colour she's chosen as
dye of the month. 'It's a losing battle, boy,' she moans. You think
I'd have inherited something better than the grey hair gene from
my mother, but no—no.'

At home, Auntie's always in shapeless loud caftans that make
her look fatter than she is with rounded bits sticking out here
and there. Her breasts are droopy. Often, she hugs me and it is a
warm, soft place to bury my face in because Mum is bony and it
isn't comfortable to let her hold you tight.

I slip into her house. Picasso, Auntie's mongrel pup, waylays
me. He leaps at me; I fall to the ground wrestling him away as
he pulls at my shirt, licks my face and finally stands on me, all
the time barking like the mad dog he is. It's a daily ritual. Picasso
(because he's the ugliest dog ever) knows I love him to bits but
there's a gnawing in my insides when I see Auntie kiss him or
when he jumps onto Uncle's lap. My eyes stop smiling, I can't help
it. In a moment, Uncle crooks his finger at me. I jump onto his
lap as well. Picasso protests indignantly and wrestles me for the
comfiest spot. We soon settle in, me on Uncle's lap, Picasso on
mine and Uncle's arms around us both.

Auntie brings me toast and eggs and makes me a hot Milo.
'Eat, eat. You won't be hungry so long as I am here.' Her voice is
indignant.

'Thanks, Auntie.' Mum's very particular about good manners.
'I don't know where Dad's gone. Woke up this morning and he
wasn't there.'

Auntie turns to Uncle: 'GONE THE WHOLE NIGHT.
THE MOST IRRESPONSIBLE PARENTS . . . '

It's not that, not really. Auntie doesn't understand, not the way I do. Mum works all hours taking on overtime every single day so when she returns home, she's only good for a quick meal in a stall somewhere, a bit of TV and then bed. Dad works just as hard. I usually try to get in all my school news and requests at dinner. They listen with half a mind; if I reach out to touch them, I can almost feel the bone-crunching fatigue that flows from their bodies and washes away their appetites and smiles.

Weekends, Mum can hardly steer out of bed, for she's got to face the washing and cleaning and tidying and cooking so going to Klang is a real treat for her.

See, she's the youngest in her family. When she goes to her brother's, Mum's a little girl again. Her voice is just a wee bit squeaky with a lisp. She talks and laughs like some of the silly girls in my class, forever sucking up to the teacher. Mum and her brother, they cook their favourite dishes, then sit and chat and watch TV. She's always so contented like she's in a safe place where she's completely taken care of. A place where she doesn't need to make difficult decisions.

If she's not there, she goes shopping. She's got wheels on her feet, Mum has. She can't stop at a place for long, especially if that place is home.

I finish breakfast and help Auntie wash up. I play with Picasso. Maybe I'm delaying returning home. Home is silence even with the TV on at full blast. Home is dirty dishes in the sink and on the dining table. Clothes lying everywhere, overcrowding the laundry basket, newly washed clothes spilling over the chairs, falling over the sofa, covering the beds. Clothes Mum has no time to fold. I can deal with the small stuff but the shirts and blouses are way beyond me.

I'm not complaining, mind you. After all, Mum did ask me to stay back with her in Klang. Dad pushed me to stay too. But I wanted my own bed. I remember Dad being silent the whole journey back home; he didn't once talk to me. His mobile rang. He barked: 'I'll be there! Give me fifteen minutes!'

When we reached home, I was nodding off. He picked me up gently enough and carried me to my bed. He tucked the blanket around me and kissed me. I stirred. He hushed me. He switched on the night light. I was out already. Then I woke up this morning and he wasn't there.

'I'll go back home now, Auntie,' I announce.

She grins. 'Maybe I should adopt you so I can look after you properly.'

'You are already looking after me, Auntie. You're my second Mum.' Then I casually bend down to scratch Picasso under his jaw. Obliging, he licks my face so my voice is muffled. 'See, I got to look after them.'

Well, Auntie's got sharp ears too. As I climb back over the fence, her whispery voice floats up loud and clear. 'NINE YEARS OLD—AND HOW COME HE'S SO MATURE AND HIS PARENTS ARE NOT?'

Dear Auntie. There are things she doesn't understand, perhaps because she doesn't have children herself.

Like how my Mum's eyes are too often sad or my Dad's shift here and there, his brows knitted in a straight line. Like how they both scurry around everywhere and fill their spaces with anything on hand so they won't need to spend time together. I have to take care of them. There's no one else.

Dad returns home. Oh goody, he's carrying a packet of nasi lemak. I smile broadly as I unlock the gate.

'Hey you!' He rumples my hair. 'Up already? I went for a walk this morning. Thought you'd still be sleeping when I got back.'

My mouth stretches so wide it hurts. His bed wasn't slept in. He's wearing the same shirt and pants as he was last night. He isn't sweating one bit after the walk and I catch a whiff of something like faded perfume.

'We'll go to Klang this afternoon and fetch your Mum, okay?'
Dad puts his arm around my shoulders as we walk to the house.

'Sure, Dad.'

I can sense Auntie behind her door grill. I can almost hear
her snort.

END

9

Will You Let Him Drink the Wind?

Kannan can't speak. Can't brush his teeth, bathe or wash his bum. Can't button his shirt, pull up his pants or feed himself. Can walk though. He never stops walking. Can make little grunts and sing-song noises; never not makes them. Kannan isn't lovable, there lies the problem. After I'm dead and the husband too, who will love my son? It is easier to love cute and adorable, no? Kannan is neither. Someone will give him a home, I'm sure of it. We are a large, close-knit family. There will be a place for him somewhere. Someone will feed him and clothe him and give him a bed to sleep, of that I'm certain.

But God, who will dance with him? Take him for walks where he runs downhill, ungraceful on his spindly legs and flat feet, making little sounds of pleasure, laughing with his mouth wide open so you can see all his teeth. Who will wait with him awhile, when he, standing for a minute, head cocked to a side, listens to a song no one can hear, swinging his body to the left, to the right, faster and faster till you feel light-headed just watching him.

Who will seat him on the playground swing, this six-foot tall baby, and push him to the skies so he clutches the ropes tight and drinks the wind on his face?

Who will not beat him, God, please, not beat him, when he soils his pants twice in five minutes because he refuses to sit on the commode for longer than ten seconds? If they hit him, he will be bewildered. My heart bleeds that unloving hands should touch him so.

The crux of the matter is: babies are adorable. Toddlers are cute. Adult-disabled are not. And as you know, Kannan is pushing 29, still unable to do just about anything on his own. His dad shaves him once every two days. Kannan has calluses on his hands and feet; at times spittle drools from his mouth or a glob of mucous peeps from his nostril. He does not know how to blow his nose. He hates to be touched though he will hold your hand—usually to pull you to the dining table so you can feed him or to the CD player so you can put on the only CD he will ever listen to, Pithukuli's Kannan songs. Bless you, Pithukuli—you create happy places inside him. You call out, 'Kanna! Kanna!' and my son's face lifts into a broad, happy grin and he dances. He spins on the floor in frantic ecstasy.

Coming back, some people get unnerved when Kannan grabs their hand—and I understand their discomfort perfectly. Why should they be expected to like, love, embrace a person simply because he is disabled? That's my point, you do see it don't you, God, that when it comes to people loving Kannan, choices are limited. And he doesn't help in any way. Self-focused like a baby. Always me-me-me. Feed me. Feed me. Feed me. Or play my songs on the CD player. You can be lying down with a blinding headache in a darkened room; along he comes to pull you up or nuzzle your face till his spittle and sweat mingle on your cheek. If you still resist, he will piss in his pants. You can be hunched over your laptop desperately trying to complete your copy because the design people across town are calling every ten minutes for it, when he tugs at your hand and you shoo him away and he tugs and tugs and your concentration gets shot to bits . . . Will they, who take care of him, live with that, God?

Or will they lock him up in a distant room away from everyone. He'll be scared, God. He can't bear to be shut up alone. He bangs the door and shrieks down the house. It is not wilfulness, you know, just fear. Will they understand? That he deliberately pushes all your buttons because . . . no reason really.

His dad and I are his parents. We love him and we look out for him. I can't help thinking though, God, what a high price it is that his brother has to pay or his cousins, for being forced in future to take care of him. What a high price for being family. Surely, duty should not come with such heavy responsibility. For it will be a burden, make no mistake about it.

So, here's the deal, God. You made him—now, now, don't give us the karma stuff. Karma is acceptable only when it happens to other people. Especially don't spin us that stuff about how 'God gives to those who can'. When I hear those words, I want to punch the person in the face. What smug trivializing of lives altered forever. Kannan may be the most helpless, most dependent being in our household; he is also the most powerful. Every single routine, schedule, decision in our lives is governed by him.

A long time ago, when Kannan was a beautiful-faced child, Jean, an ex-colleague, told me with all righteous Christian fervour, 'God looks around for a special home for his special children and he has chosen you. Mind you, you are blessed indeed.'

I told her, 'Let's share the blessedness, Jean. Tell you what, you keep him for the weekend. I don't mind. You keep him, stay awake the whole night because he sleeps in fits and snatches and when he's awake, he'll tear at his diapers, leaving trails of piss-soaked clumps of gel and cotton while he tramples all over the house, upstairs and downstairs. You go on, keep him, brush his teeth, give him his bath, wash his bum, feed him and give over your peace to non-stop shrieks and noises and grunts—after all, it is only for a weekend. Watch the blessed silence fly out of the window. Will you do that, Jean?'

Jean glared at me as if she could not believe her ears at the words of this unnatural mother. But she said nothing, God, she said nothing. And while we are on it, what's with all these women coming to me and saying: 'Did you feel angry when you first found out? Surely you must have asked, 'Why me?' I tell them, 'Why not me? You mean to say only certain people should have disabled kids and I shouldn't? You mean some people, me included, should be *exempted*?' They back away and mutter, 'Boy, talk about anger issues.'

Of course, I am angry. I mean why disabled kids, God? Why? Have you had a look at one recently? Don't tell me it's because we can learn to be better parents—you do know babies are dumped every day, don't you? If I need to learn, let me suffer and learn. Why the heck should my child be born disabled so that I can learn to be a better parent? It sounds like the height of arrogance, if you ask me.

So, God, here's the deal. We love him; you know that, don't you? What I am going to say, I earned the right to say, ok?

You take him, God, before us. Well before us. Before we lose the strength in our limbs to care for him properly. Before by his constant never-ending demands, he leaches away our love for him from our souls. You take him. It is unbearable that after us, Kannan should be suffered as a duty to be endured, just because he's family. Give him some respect, God. Surely he's entitled to that. I worry that they won't know him beyond his not-so-lovable face. They won't know that when he's very quiet, it means he's ill. Something's hurting, whether it is his head or stomach or maybe he's injured himself. They won't know, God. They might sigh with relief and say 'Thank God he's still'.

Kannan can't speak, true, but when he drinks the wind and holds music in his body, he's singing songs we can't understand. Or in pain and lying still, eyes looking inward to the source, he's speaking words we can't hear. His dad and I are the two constants in his life; when we are gone, he'll think we've abandoned him. And he'll be afraid and unable to express it. Doesn't bear thinking about. Leave him some dignity, for God's sake. That, he deserves. Over to you, God.

END

10

Woman in the Mirror

Kamala knew the old woman was a snarky piece of work, always sneaking into the mirror to lie in wait for her. She was always doing that. The main thing was to never, ever look into the mirror. But that evening, Kamala was fifteen years old and she forgot. So, she went into the bathroom to take a shower, took off her blouse, unhooked her bra, and—glancing at the mirror, she screamed. And kept screaming, unable to look away because the old woman was undressed just like her, with the same bra hanging loose, and in exactly the same sarong, doing exactly what Kamala was doing—screaming.

She had a strong chiselled face, black hair flecked with grey; dark eyebrows. The lines around her eyes were etched deeply because her eyes were open wide like Kamala's and as they both screamed, Kamala felt her face cracking and breaking into exactly seventy-two pieces which she knew by instinct was the woman's age. She knelt down, scrambled for them on the floor, desperate to find the pieces and fix them back between her ears when she felt warm pee run between her legs, splash on her sarong and slosh into a puddle on the floor.

Frantic, Kamala tugged off her sarong. Maybe she could bundle it into the washing machine before the madam spotted it. It fell into the puddle. She picked it up. It was dripping wet.

The weight of it all. It crushed her. One thing after another, again and again. Sundran would know what to do but Kamala couldn't find him anymore. He was gone, just like that. *Where are you, my brother*, she thought, with a hurt that clenched her heart. *This is a nightmare house, Sundran. An old woman hides in mirrors. The landlady calls me 'mother-in-law'—can you imagine? Me? There are no exits here— I've looked. Save me, Sundran. Sundran.*

Her chest was going to burst. Overwhelmed, she leaned against the wash basin and began to weep. That was how they found her, weeping, her sarong in a heap around her feet, her breath ragged as she strained to breathe.

'You okay, Amma?' Ranjan said.

'Why are you half-naked?' Susheela drawled. 'You peed in your sarong again, didn't you, Athai? Tsk, tsk.'

'For God's sake, madam, stop calling me mother-in-law,' Kamala groaned. Turning her back on Susheela, she grabbed the nice man's hands. 'I can't find my Sundran. Please sir, I want my brother.'

'Your brother Sundran is dead. Dead for over fifty years.' Susheela said.

'Liar, liar, pants on fire!' Kamala burst out, refusing to wipe away the hot tears that stung her eyes.

'I'll cover all the mirrors, Amma. You won't see the old woman again. Promise.' Ranjan said.

'Come, let's get you to the shower, Athai. You'll be clean in no time.' Susheela's voice was soft.

* * *

The next morning, freshly showered once again, wearing a crisp cotton saree, ignoring the pain in her chest, Kamala stood in the garden, watching the river lap the edges where earth met water. The river meandered along, almost parallel to the street on the other side. She had lived by the river all her life; first, with her brother Sundran and her father and later, her husband. Not in this house but another, just a few minutes away. She remembered her father yelling at Sundran the moment her typewriter began clacking first thing in the morning. *You're ruining her life. Filling her head with ideas. Writing stories—who's going to marry her, boy?* And Sundran's retort: *Someone who'll value her brain as well, not just her pretty face.* Hah, that turned out *pretty well*, didn't it?

Where was that house I grew up in? For a few seconds she peered down the river before shaking her head. *That way lies madness, woman. Get a grip. It is not the same river. My house was in Mambang, another town, by another river, in another world, and besides they are dead, all of them.*

I'm the keeper of our histories. How else will I keep Sundran alive? Not the others, but Sundran. It was Sundran who had bought her first typewriter, sent her stories to magazines, who was ecstatic when they got published. Not her father, and later, not her husband. Knowledge had frightened them and learning in a woman had sent them berserk. She remembered the desperate hide-and-seek they played, as she hid her manuscripts from father and husband, always one step ahead of hands that searched to destroy. *Sure*, she thought, *I could have left my husband, but no one ever did such things those days. Besides, where could I have gone? To Sundran? He was gone by then. To my father? He'd have sent me right back to the husband.*

'Why can't you be an ordinary wife?' The husband had raged before hitting her. And hitting her and hitting because she wouldn't cry. Or bend to him. And wouldn't stop writing. What did her father and husband look like? She couldn't remember their faces. She couldn't remember her husband's name.

She thought of the large shadowy patches in her mind, like shrouds that leaped and jeered at her just beyond her reach. Did shrouds leap? She had no idea. They danced more erratically now, usurping more of her memories. Someone, a neighbour maybe, must have reported to Ranjan and he came one morning to Mambang, locked up her house and took her to live with him.

She did try to tell him, *I can't stay with you, son. Your wife will drive me crazy.* She thought he'd smile at that. He didn't but his eyes glinted. *Look at it this way, Amma. With any luck, you'll each drive the other mad. It's just a matter of who goes under first.*

Susheela. That was her name. When he introduced her at lunch one day, as the girl he was going to marry, Kamala tried to make her laugh, as if to tell her she was willing to be her friend. She didn't smile, didn't laugh. She knew the calories and the nutritional value of the dishes they were having, though. Towards the end of the meal, Kamala remarked, looking directly at Ranjan, *Well, that was the nicest plate of shredded glass I've ever eaten.* She was rude, she knew. His face turned pale. Then Susheela said in her flat voice, *True. Nice bowl of glass noodles, not shredded glass. Two laps around the school field to burn it all off.*

Why he wanted to marry her, his mother had no idea. She was hurt, to tell the truth, for surely, he could have found someone like her: animated, lively, creative. Why she wanted to marry him was obvious of course. Anybody would have wanted to marry him.

Kamala stood a little longer looking at the river and seeing the shrouds at play, jumping around, yelling in glee. *So, this is how it is going to be. A descent into the relentless. Soon, I won't recognize Ranjan and Susheela. Will I scream and yell all the time? Or will I smile and be just plain batty? Will I torture these two people till they hate me?*

She heard the sound of footsteps behind her and smelt coffee. Ranjan joined her, carrying a mug. He handed it to her, his hand holding hers carefully until she had the mug safely. 'Son, promise me if I ever totally lose my marbles, you'll shoot me.'

'I don't have a gun, Amma.'

'Oh, that's right, I forgot. Stab me with a knife, then.'

He gave her a glum look. 'Don't know how. Have to practise.'

'Hmm.' She thought for a bit and shook her head. 'No, a knife would hurt too much. How about sleeping pills?'

'On top form today, are we, Kamala Balan?' he murmured, smiling.

She tried to return the smile but it wavered. 'So, sleeping pills. Fifty or so should do the trick,' she continued.

Placing his arm around her shoulders, Ranjan led her back to the house. 'Fifty pills? I don't know where to get that many. The pharmacy, you think? Maybe I could forge a prescription. If only I knew one of those drug dealers . . . '

Susheela heard him. 'He'll get them, give them to you and go to jail. That's what you want? He's fifty-two years old; won't last a week in jail, not with those bad knees. How about jumping into the river, Athai? It's just two minutes from here.'

'Gee, thanks, I'll keep it in mind.' Kamala grimaced.

'Susheela,' Ranjan sighed.

'I feel as if chunks of my memories are wrapped in shrouds and I can't get to them. I saw them dancing just now . . . ' Kamala's voice was low but Susheela heard her and pounced on her words. 'That's why Athai, I say you need time alone—to reflect, to remember—and who knows, maybe even to write once again. The nursing home will be ideal. Just for a month, see? Until we come back from Europe. Go on, give it a chance.'

'Susheela,' Ranjan said.

'It's not fair, Ranjan. We planned this trip for ages. Three weeks in Europe. I've shopped for it, dreamed of it and now when we're about to leave, you say we can't. Not fair, you know.'

'I can't leave my mother. Not now.'

'You'd better go with her, son. Or she'll moan and whine till the day you die.'

'I'm not whining.'

'Of course, you are,' Kamala snapped. 'God knows how you teach your students. You probably nag and moan and whine at them till they mug like mad, pass their exams . . . do anything to get you off their backs.'

'You could come with us, Amma,' Ranjan said hurriedly. 'We could do Europe together, all three of us.'

Susheela's mouth dropped open. Kamala grinned. 'Good idea. She'll do nothing but shop all day and we will have to tag along to each store, one after another, until I die of ennui. Good thinking, son.'

'You horrid, dreadful woman! You ruin everything. I wish you'd never come to stay with us.' Susheela turned to Ranjan. 'I can't do this, Ranjan. I have a right to my life. A. Happy. Peaceful. Life.'

Kamala listened to her going on at it till she was bored. She raised her eyes and there he was, sitting in a small photograph on the wall. 'I hope you are happy now, old man. Everything is your fault.'

'Who are you talking to, Amma?'

'Him. My father.'

'No Amma. He's *my* father.'

'Oh, he's your father too?' She gazed at Ranjan with wonder. He looked at her with an expression she couldn't understand. Susheela took her arm. 'Come, Athai. Breakfast. Idli and tomato chutney. I'll give you your medication after that. The number of pills you and your son take, you could open your own pharmacy. Two sickly people. Oh my God.'

'Don't worry. We'll share the pills with you and you can join the club.'

* * *

It was a good breakfast. Feeling bad about teasing Susheela, Kamala agreed to visit the Florence Nightingale Nursing Home— *just to have a look, mind.* Susheela was ecstatic. Her face actually grew animated. 'It's barely five minutes by car. We'll leave right away, after we're done with breakfast.' She couldn't wait. It wounded the older woman.

'This is the end, then,' she said. 'A lifetime fighting to keep my own voice, trying to transcend the utter stupidity of people who had all the power over me, and in the end, every single thing gets reduced to black holes in my mind and a deluxe room in the Florence Nightingale Nursing Home. With an attached bath. The end.'

'That's not the end,' Susheela looked up from her plate. 'Death is the end,' she announced. Kamala tried, she really tried but no, she couldn't bite down the wasp in her tongue. 'You would have got along famously with my father and my husband. They were just as literal.'

'No, Amma. You don't get to say that to her.' Ranjan's voice was firm.

'That's all right, Ranjan,' Susheela said. 'Let her say what she wants. I can be magnanimous.'

'Because I'm leaving?'

'Exactly.' Susheela smiled but her eyes were moist.

'What an irony,' Kamala remarked. 'My mind is going and I don't know how to put an end to it all.' She took a deep breath. 'So, family, here I am, a once famous award-winning writer, with dozens of stories to my name—' She stopped. Susheela was rolling her eyes.

'What?'

'You've written a grand total of fourteen short stories and one novel, Athai. You won a magazine award at seventeen for being the most promising teen writer but your last two stories came out thirty years ago. After that—nothing. *Nada. Nil. Rien. Nichts. Nyet.*'

Kamala stared at her. Yes, Susheela had certainly been practising for going to Europe. Still, whatever else she did, her daughter-in-law did not tell lies. 'I'm not a famous writer?'

Susheela shook her head. 'Once you were. No longer.' She steadfastly refused to look at Ranjan, who was sitting next to his mother, making all kinds of frantic gestures. 'You haven't been published in thirty years.'

'Oh.' There was silence for a while. Kamala did not know what to say. Her chest was hurting a bit more.

'You told me the most wonderful stories when I was growing up, Amma,' Ranjan said. 'You were always telling me stories, and not just at bedtime. You'd be grinding rice for thosai—you remember the stone grinder, humongous granite wasn't it? From the Neolithic Age probably—and I'd be helping you and listening to all the stories that sprang as if fully formed from inside you. You were a natural teller of stories, Amma.'

'Why didn't I write them down?'

'You tried. You wrote and wrote every day, but they didn't come out so well. You kept tearing up the paper and trying again and again, getting more and more angry each time. And then . . . there was Appa . . . if he found your stories, he burned them . . . and there'd be a fight.'

'So, the past thirty years, I've written nothing? Nothing?' she asked Ranjan.

His face was kind. 'Nothing, Amma.'

She felt an infinite sadness creep over her. So, her memory was a traitor too, just like Sundran who had died, taking away almost everything that was of value in her life. *What else was it lying about,* she wondered. 'Tell me,' she asked, hesitant, 'Did your father ever beat me?'

Ranjan's face was bleak. After a while he whispered, 'Not after I was old enough—to stop him.'

'I remember that.' She squeezed her son's hand. 'I remember all of that. Even as a child, you'd jump on him and grab his hand that was going to hit me and place it on your head. He could never hurt you.' She was silent with the remembering. 'He said I diminished him. Took away his manhood.'

Ranjan reached out and touched his mother's face. 'You were no good for each other. Marriage for life—it was a prison sentence for him too, Amma.'

She wasn't going to concede that. 'We lived in different spaces in the same house, but everywhere I went, you could cut the rage with a knife.'

'You. Could. Have. Left. Him.' Susheela spoke to the chutney bowl, her eyebrows arched, till they almost reached her hairline.

'You didn't do divorce those days, Susheela!' Kamala protested. 'You just put up with it.'

'Yeah, right.' This time, Susheela's eyes bored into her mother-in-law's. 'Sure.'

Kamala swallowed hard. She glanced at Ranjan. He was gesturing to his wife to shut up. Susheela's eyes never left her.

'All right, all right, I was a coward, okay? Happy now? I didn't know where to go, what to do. Sundran was dead. My father would have sent me back to the husband. And I had my son . . . '

'So, you put up with it and *he* put up with both of you every single day,' Susheela snapped, tilting her head at Ranjan. 'You didn't think of that, did you? So now you know why we chose not to have children.'

'Susheela, no!' Ranjan closed his eyes.

Kamala felt as if a hand was pushing her deep into a pool of water and relentless, wouldn't let her go. She struggled to breathe. 'What's she saying?' she turned to Ranjan. 'You didn't want to have children? Because of your father and me? Ranjan!'

Ranjan looked at her. She searched his face. There was no anger in it, just acceptance. 'Every single time when the three of us were in a room together, when we were eating or watching TV, I would be in a state, waiting for one of you to start yelling to begin a fight. Then I had to watch out that he didn't hit you or you didn't cut him with your tongue or smash too many plates and

when the noise rose higher and higher, I would run around trying
to push you out of the room or get Appa away from you.

'I couldn't bear to have children in case I put them through
the same thing.'

Each word he said fell like a stone on her heart. She thought
she would collapse with the pain. She gulped for air. 'You were the
one person in my life who kept me sane, Ranjan,' she cried, a sob
rising from her throat. 'I would have given my life for you without
a second thought over and over again . . . and all the time, all the
bloody time . . . Oh God,' she covered her head with her hands.
'You were a child . . . What kind of monsters were we?'

'Don't go there, Amma. It's in the past.' His voice became terse.

'But you were a child, Ranjan!' She couldn't keep the horror
from her voice. 'Your father and I, we never thought . . . We hated
each other. All we thought about was how we could hurt each
other. It sustained us,' she spluttered. 'All through the marriage,
it was the hate that made it bearable. We never thought about
you . . . '

'Hush, hush, no more of that, Amma. Give it a rest. I loved
you and I loved Appa—separately.'

'Still,' Kamala could not let it rest. 'I didn't know . . . '

'Stop it.' He rounded on her. 'How could you not know? My
earliest memories—you know what they are—not of a teddy bear
or toys or kisses. My earliest memories—you yelling at him, him
hitting you, you falling on the ground and me, me, jumping on you
and covering you with my body. You know how old I was?' He
rasped at her. 'Maybe two, maybe three . . . a freaking kid, that's all
I know. I don't think I knew to talk. I remember crying though.'

He was quiet for a while. 'A freaking kid with the most self-
absorbed, most selfish arses as parents. And I loved you. Now,
give it a rest please.'

She did not open her mouth. What was there to say? Susheela,
quiet for all of ten seconds, shrugged. 'I was okay with not having

kids. Get enough of them in school. Don't need to live with them at home.' She let off a big sigh. 'And now, people,' she got up from her chair. 'I'm going to get dressed. One of us has to impress the matron of Florence Nightingale and it's not going to be either of you.'

They watched her go. Kamala's mind was clear. The shrouds were gone for the moment. 'I'm sorry. I'm so sorry, son.'

'Me too, Amma.'

She looked at her beautiful boy. Suddenly it was vital to tell him she hadn't always been that horrid self-centred woman; that once she used to laugh and sing and dance but the words came out broken and disjointed although they were clear in her mind.

He hushed her again. They sat without speaking. Then Ranjan pushed his chair closer to hers. Presently, he asked, 'He died of a fever, didn't he?' She knew who he meant. To her utter astonishment, her lips trembled and she began to weep. 'Just a bit of fever, that was all and the next morning, Sundran was dead. Dead! He was bloody twenty-six!' she howled. 'I wouldn't let them take him. I held on to his body and screamed when they tried to pull me away.' She touched the tears on her cheeks. 'They had to prise me away from him. Then my father refused to wait till the mourning was over. He got me married almost immediately.'

'Why on earth?'

'It was the letter from the university, see. University of Malaya in Singapore. I had a place to read English and he was afraid I would go.' Kamala covered her face with her hands, trying to mask the sound of her sobs, now loud and wild, uncontrollable.

Ranjan got up from his chair. He knelt down and put his arms around her.

'I can't believe I'm crying over something that happened more than fifty years ago!' She tried to laugh. 'How crazy is that?' He held her without speaking. 'After all this time, it still has the power . . . ' she struck her breast, 'to annihilate me . . . '

They held each other in silence before Ranjan stood up.
'Blasted knees.' He sat back on his chair.

'I never wept for your father,' she said presently. 'When they
brought him home from hospital for the funeral, I couldn't cry.
Your grandfather wept—like a baby. And you too. I—I was
thinking, I'm free, I'm free, I'm free, free to finally do what I
want but I didn't know the rage was already like a fire in my
heart, burning everything down to ash. I couldn't write anymore.
Everything was gone except the hate.' She looked at her son. 'And
now when I'm about to die . . . ' He shook his head. She said, 'I'm
not *afraid* of death, Ranjan.'

'No. Just a gateway, isn't it?'

'Yes. And then rebirth—and a new adventure. No, death isn't
scary; it's my journey towards it . . . ' She thought for a bit. 'I'm
terrified of not remembering anymore. That I can't fill all the gaps
in my memories. And that it will get worse and far worse. I feel
as if I'm standing on quicksand and the ground is shifting as we
speak.' She felt her smile twist her lips. 'Oh God, how banal. The
utter bloody banality of it all.'

'Kamala Balan!' Ranjan leaned across and kissed her. 'Even if
you went totally gaga, you would never be banal! Trust me.'

* * *

Susheela was still getting dressed when Ranjan went upstairs to
collect his car keys and wallet. Left alone, Kamala walked about,
her hand pressed hard on her breast. The pain was spreading; she
thought she would keel over from it. She couldn't breathe. She
needed fresh air. She moved as rapidly as she could towards the
front door, past a mirror in the hallway and had almost reached
the door when she paused and doubled back. The woman in the
mirror looked back at her, her face reddened and swollen like hers.
A raw guttural grief tore through Kamala's lungs. She touched the
mirror with both hands. The other woman responded and for a

few moments, they were both wrapped in a silence that bound them together and then released her completely.

When she stumbled out of the house a little later, she found herself in the garden. The outside felt different. The road was gone, the river was broader, and her old house from Mambang peeped from around the corner. She stood still, focusing all her thoughts on it, willing it to stay and not disappear. At that moment, the old shrouds appeared, mocking as usual, dancing closer and closer, their black skeletal fingers waving, reaching out to pluck out more pieces of her brain.

They blocked her view of her house. She pushed them away; instead, they pressed closer. She pushed them away again but they grew stronger, denser and she felt a huge dread engulf her, about to swallow her whole.

Sundran! Sundran! She cried out and then there he was, standing by the river a few yards away, smiling at her, looking exactly as she'd known him all her life, dressed in khaki pants and a shirt with the sleeves folded up. Leather shoes on his feet and a grin on his face and his hair just a little long, needing a barber's touch. All at once, she knew he was real and all the shrouds mere figments of imagination. At that knowing, they vanished.

'Kamala!' Sundran beckoned to her. She shook her head like a petulant teenager.

'Where did you go, huh, all these years? I looked everywhere for you, you know.'

His face turned sober. 'I had to go, Kamala. It wasn't my choice. You want to come now? With me?' He beckoned again.

Oh no, she wasn't going to let him off so easily. 'All these years, you're gone, then you come back, you wag your finger and you expect me to come running just like that? Nah. You don't know what happened to me, Sundran . . . '

His gaze tore her heart. 'I know, rajathi.' Rajathi. He was the only person to call her that, his little princess. She didn't realize how much she'd missed that loving.

'You were not here to make it different, Sundran,' she cried. 'Where did you go where did you go *where did you go?*'

He held his arms out without speaking.

'You're going away again, aren't you?' she asked, dread in her voice.

He smiled at her and it was as if the sun came out at that moment. 'Not without you, rajathi!' When she heard him, the pain in her chest lifted. He held his arms out again and nodded. Laughing with relief, she ran towards him, her steps sure-footed like a young girl's. Somewhere, she heard a man cry out and a woman shouting, 'No, Ranjan, don't run. You can't run, remember your knees!'

Ranjan did not run. He strode briskly towards his mother. She was rattling the padlocked gates trying to push them open. He heard her sob, 'Wait for me Sundran! Don't you dare disappear again, you hear?' When he reached her, he touched her lightly on her shoulder and called, 'Kamala Balan!' She turned around, her face drenched, though with tears or sweat he could not say. When she saw who it was, a smile of utter happiness lit up her face. Her arms went around him and as she slumped against him, Ranjan knew that neither smile nor embrace were for him.

END

11

When We Are Young

When I got up this morning and unmuted the phone, I knew there would be a couple of missed calls from Hsian and Arun. There were seven: two from Arun from yesterday evening and five from Hsian. I wasn't in any mood to call back. *Die, Arun. Die. Die.* He'd probably wanted to blether an apology while Hsian— well, he was always playing peacemaker between Arun and me, what else was new?

'We've been friends for too long, come on, Farida,' he'd say.

And I'd say, 'Friends? He's no friend, Hsian, not any longer. What kind of friend calls you those dreadful ugly names?'

More than anger was Arun's treachery. It ate into me, a parasite tunnelling into my brain. Arun had always been more than a neighbour; he'd been my brother, far more than my own. And I'd thought he'd felt the same way about me. Yesterday though, all friendships had come undone, ripped and shredded until I thought I'd die from the pain, the pain. *Die, Arun, die.*

Hsian rang again twice—I ignored the calls—while I was having breakfast with Abah. Just the two of us, the way I liked. My mother and Kak Minah were in the kitchen discussing lunch. My brother Zul didn't believe in early breakfasts on weekends. He was still in his room. I could hear him make waking-up sounds. He was something else, that boy; yesterday evening, he was suddenly all subdued, all stricken. He'd come home after a rough game of football, with his jersey bloodied and torn. He went to bed without his dinner. Then, when I came down to the kitchen for a drink in the middle of the night, I found him burning his jersey at the sink. I mean who destroys an original Man U jersey? He looked at me and shook his head. Okay, okay, no questions. I had my problems, he had his.

My phone rang again. 'Answer the phone,' Abah said. It was Hsian, still playing peacemaker. I geared myself to do battle.

'Don't talk to me about Arun, Hsian,' I snapped by way of 'hello'. 'He's dead to me, understand?'

Except Hsian began sobbing. 'We're at the hospital. Arun . . . Arun is . . . '

He broke down and I found myself screaming: 'Arun? Hsian! ARUN!'

My father took the phone from my hand and found out what had happened. I must have shrieked so loudly that Mak and Kak Minah came running from the kitchen. Even Zul rushed out of his room. I couldn't stop the screaming until Abah said Arun was in the hospital and he'd drive me there. No questions, just a statement: 'He's alive, Farida.' That's my Abah.

Mak did try to stop us. 'Hold on, she can't go. She's got no business at the hospital. She's not family.' Kak Minah fixed her with a beady look. 'As far as I know, right from kindergarten, this girl has been going straight to Arun's house after school. She eats there, does her homework there, spends all her time there, coming back here just to bathe, pray and sleep.' Her face was grim. 'She's family all right, believe me.' Kak Minah, our maid, was our de facto ruler of the household. My mother knew that if we didn't please her, she'd leave us and return to Indonesia.

In the car, Abah asked in his soft voice, 'What happened between you and Arun, Farida?'

'I don't want to talk about it,' I said, before blurting out, 'We quarrelled. He got an offer from the university.'

'Engineering?'

'No.' My voice was low. 'Consumer Studies.'

'Consumer what?' Abah looked at me. 'He scored 3As in his *STPM* and gets Consumer whatsit. Hell. You scored 3As in your A-levels and you got dentistry in Australia on a full scholarship.' He gave a little bark. 'The perks of being the right race in this country.'

Not my Abah too. I closed my eyes.

* * *

So here I am in the hospital, trying to block out the smell of disease that hovers in the air, not quite masked by strong antiseptics. It's not the cheeriest of places. I'm looking at Arun. Head injuries. Broken ribs. I hope he burns in hell, whoever did this to my friend. Tubes link his bandaged chest, arms, and a finger to drips and machines. I feel a rush of tenderness and it takes me by surprise.

'I mean, dude,' I tell him silently, 'all these years, if I ever wasted brain space on you, it was because you were my *macha* next door. Of course, I also thought of that *monyet*, Hsian who is now blubbering next to you. Okay, okay, I admit I spent far more time thinking of him than you. In my soppiest moments I've even doodled, *Farida heart Hsian. Heart. Heart.* Yesterday morning—was it only yesterday?—I never ever wanted to lay eyes on you again, and now, look—' a sob escapes from my throat—'I'm at your side, crying and all astonished that I'm crying, macha!' My face aches with the unaccustomed crying.

I turn to look at Auntie Ruku and Hsian, their hands gentle on Arun's body as if their touch with the weight of all their love would surely bring him back from the brink. More than anything I want to run to them, feel the warmth of Auntie Ruku's embrace, but I hold back. Instead, I turn to Arun again and continue my silent conversation with him.

'Hey, Arun, guess what? I met some of your *well-wishers* outside the ward. They were muttering: "Why is she here, that Melayu girl? His girlfriend, ah? Cannot get any Indian girl? I hear the Malays beat him up. All useless. Drug addicts. Not enough the Malays did this to him, he's got a Malay girl and she wants him to convert, izzit? And that Cheenen? What's he doing here? No Indian friend, ah?"

'I turned to them, not caring if my words cut like a razor. *Not girlfriend. Kawan lah. Geddit?* They wouldn't. No matter. Adults are all idiots, including this lot, and anyway, I'm not budging from your side. Hsian isn't either. And certainly not Auntie Ruku.'

The room is quiet except for the beep of the machines. The three of us are in separate bubbles of grief. We don't talk to each other yet the unspoken tension crackles beneath the surface. I expect anytime now for Auntie Ruku to tell me to get lost. 'Go away girl, you never wanted to see us again, remember?' During 'the quarrel', she had tried to grab my hand only for me to shake it off, as if it were infectious.

I wait. To tell the truth, I half expect Arun to open his eyes now that we are all sitting around his bed—you know lah, that's how it always works in the movies. Cue: sad, heart-breaking music. Camera zooms into a close-up of a beautiful young girl with wet face (me) gazing at a boy in a coma in a hospital bed. Boy's eyes flicker and slowly open. He's awake! Sad music changes to a joyful tune.

Arun's not making this easy, is he? His eyes remain stubbornly closed.

'Listen, Auntie Ruku, Farida,' Hsian speaks softly. 'Let's talk to him. I'm sure he can hear us.' Hsian has dark circles hooding his eyes. When he looks at me, he appears watchful, wary just the way Uncle Foong's dog looks, waiting for the quick, sudden kick in the belly. It bewilders me.

'What to say, Hsian?' Auntie Ruku cries. 'If anything happens to him, I will die.' Her grief has shrunken her. She avoids me. It cuts me to the quick even as I know I have only myself to blame.

'I want to say something.' I speak directly to Arun. 'About my Auntie Ruku.'

Auntie Ruku murmurs, 'No need, no need.'

'She's not my aunt. She's not my race or my religion. She's no blood relative at all. *Calling her 'Auntie' just as you do is a mere gesture of respect. You don't actually have to care for her or anything.* That's what my mother tried to drum into me. No matter. From the day I first met her, I've loved Auntie Ruku. That's what I try to tell my mother but as usual, she isn't listening to me. Well, you know my mum, I'm not exactly her favourite offspring, right?'

My battles with my mother were a regular feature. I wasn't pliable like my brother Zul. I wasn't obedient like him. More importantly for her, I refused to wear the tudung like she wanted me to.

'I remember the first time I met you both. Our new neighbours. 1988. I was five. The kindergarten school bus screeched to a stop right in front of my house to offload the three of us. I could see Kak Minah, our maid, waiting at our gate. By the way, Arun, Kak Minah has been with us . . . like forever. She must be at least a hundred years old now.' Behind me, I hear Hsian turn a giggle into a snort. I hear Auntie Ruku shift in her chair.

'She was carrying Zul in her arms. Hovering at the sidewalk was an Indian woman in a strange dress.'

'Strange dress? That was a housecoat, girl. And it was new.'

'First to get down was the new boy who had just moved next door. He went straight to the Indian woman. I was climbing down the steps when that monyet Hsian . . . '

'Monyet? Moi? You lah the monkey!'

Finally! My heart sings. I continue. 'When that monyet Hsian pushed me aside and scampered down first, I fell. Kak Minah switched the baby to her other arm and yelled at me.'

'Very good, fall down some more! Always careless! Never watch where you're going!'

I bawled loudly. Hsian stood looking at me with a crimson face. Then, that strange Indian woman came and crouched in front of me, and opened her arms wide. I walked into them and she held me. She held me till I stopped crying. That moment, I just fell in love with her.'

'Fell in love?' Hsian's smile is grim. 'Girl, you literally moved in. If there'd been an extra bed, you'd have even slept in her house.'

'If she had, so what?' Auntie sniffs. 'She was always welcome. Just like you.' Auntie looks at me then. 'Hsian's mother paid me to look after him, true, but I loved him and you too. I never asked your mother for money, Farida.'

It's my face that's red now. My mother has never ever offered to pay Auntie Ruku anything in cash or kind even though she knew Auntie Ruku needed money badly; even though I ate at her place, did my homework there, watched TV there, studied my lessons there and generally spent the entire day in her house. My Abah did suggest it but Mak said: 'I'm not asking her to look after my child so why should I pay her? She wants to look after her, let her lah.'

'I love all of you,' Auntie says. 'I don't look at anybody as Chinese or Indian or Malay . . . '

Hsian places his hands on his head. His eyes go wide open. I know what he's thinking. I'm thinking the same thing too—adults are the pits in the way they practise self-deception. Racists are always other people and never themselves. He walks up to Auntie and kisses her on her head. 'Yeah, right. Wasn't it you who said that Puan Maimun is a typical lazy Malay teacher?'

I grin. Seizing the moment, I hug her from the back. 'And didn't someone we know say, "That fella, typical Chinaman, nothing straight about him except his hair"?'

Auntie laughs and turns it into a cough. I suspect most people out there are like her; some of my teachers too. Arun once got into a huge fight with a new teacher when she called an Indian boy 'mabuk keling'.

'Mabuk? Mabuk?' His voice dripped with scorn. 'Puan Latifah, it's 8.30 in the morning. How can he be drunk? How crazy is that?'

'Quiet!' Puan Latifah yelled.

Arun wouldn't be quiet. 'And why do you call us keling? You know it's a disgusting word, right? We're not keling, Puan Latifah. We're Malaysian.'

He was like that, carrying all insults like stab wounds on his body. Shitty remarks about Indians as gangsters. The blackness of Indian skin. Indian drunks. Bodoh Indians in the bottom classes. Keling was the worst; the one slur bandied about so frequently and by so many people, none of whom were ethnic Indians. Arun took them all personally, lashings on his body, day in and day out. Sometimes it made me tired.

The three of us used to talk all the time about how adults were puffed up with their own grievances, their sense of victimhood. That was their tragedy. And we—we imitated them. That was ours. Anyway, no more already! Hsian, Arun, Farida. We were going to change the script. Out with race differentiation. In with equity, respect and acceptance. How on earth we were going to do that, we had no idea. Not yet.

There's a buzz from my phone in my pocket. It's a message from Zul: *Is he all right? Please tell me he's okay.* I'm touched. Zul has never clicked with either Arun or Hsian. I text back: *Can't say yet. Still unconscious.*

'You three. People say you're very good friends but dey, they don't see how you argue, always argue—Malaysian disease lah, this lah, that lah. And you never told me what that disease is. Diabetes ah?'

Hsian smiles and shakes his head. He says, 'Auntie, you remember that time when we were talking about religion?'

'Dey, you're always arguing about religion. Made my head spin.'

I remember. I said mine was the best and the purest when Hsian made a little salute and said, 'All hail Buddhism!' That was rich, coming from an atheist.

Arun said, 'Hinduism has all the answers—that's why we have loads of crooked holy men!'

Auntie Ruku looked appalled. 'Crooked? I thought they were all saints!' And she grinned.

'They're evil *Klingons*!' Arun declared. Hsian jumped in with another salute. 'All hail the Klingons! Masters of the evil universe!'

'Evil Klingons!' Auntie remembers with a smile. She goes over to Arun and touches his head. 'It never mattered that you're not my son, not my nephew, not a relative at all—your mother was my friend. When your father died, she gave you to me to raise and went to Singapore to work as a security guard. More money in Singapore, you see, so she could support you better. Who thought she'd die in a robbery? Who thought?'

I do not breathe. I did not know this, Arun, I swear. I thought she was your mother. You called her Amma. I look at Hsian. He looks as shell-shocked as me.

'Always not enough money, however hard I tried to save my pension but you know you filled all the empty spaces in my life, Arun, until these two children came along . . . and they made me so happy, made you happy. And if you die now Arun, I will die too. That's all I want to say.'

She looks at me. 'You think this Auntie's not very clever but I tell you, your quarrel yesterday, it was not your anger doing the talking. It was your ego.' She shakes her head. 'You just wanted to demolish each other.'

That. Quarrel. We always thought we were immune to the Malaysian disease. We were the face of the brave new world, willing to fight prejudice and stare at the challenges straight in the eye. And we were going places. Arun thought he was, too.

Auntie's face turns ashen. 'This boy, so clever and so foolish. Always thinking life's so easy, can get anything just like that,' she snapped her fingers. 'Just like both of you. I told him get real, boy. You cannot compare. She'll walk into a scholarship and Hsian's father will educate him but you have to take whatever they give you in a government university—because I can't afford anything else.'

I squirm when she says that. I'm a brilliant Malay student, yes, and I deserve the generous scholarship but still, there's always the lurking guilt, knowing why things are so much easier for me. Hsian's rich. His father plans to send him to Sydney to read economics. Arun applied for engineering, computer science and physics, in the government universities. He got consumer studies.

'I'll find something else.' He tossed his head. 'When you're the wrong colour, wrong religion, you got to think on your feet or you'd be crushed into nothing. I'll be fine.' He didn't look fine. I should have zipped up, right? I opened my mouth.

'Itulah,' I said with a laugh. 'If only your name was Harun instead of Arun. You'd be waltzing into a scholarship just like me.'

'YOU THINK IT IS FUNNY?' He snarled at me.

'No, I didn't mean it that way, come on man . . .' I felt flustered.

'Chill macha, chill,' Hsian stepped in.

'Don't tell me to chill, Hsian. You have no idea how I feel . . . This colour, this race, this face, this black skin . . . ' He beat his chest with his open palm. Slap. Slap. Slap. ' . . . like being forever third class.'

'Sucks big time but we're going to change it, remember?' Hsian said.

'How, Hsian? They won't let us. You know how many interviews I've gone for? So, I can get a scholarship to a private university? Huh? Got enough rejections to bury me alive.' His voice rose. 'Look at my results—they couldn't even give me physics. Consumer studies. What the heck is that? Hussein got

Engineering—bloke can't even add up properly, come on! Fatimah got veterinary science. Hah—the girl who runs a mile when she sees a dog.' He turned to me, his voice bitter. 'Your kind—you don't even have to study—it just gets handed to you on a plate.'

'My kind? My kind?' I couldn't believe my ears. *Was this my best friend speaking? Did it all in the end come down to this? My kind. Versus yours.* I felt a blinding fury surge through me.

What did I say? I remember fragments from both of us. 'You despise my kind? Go back to your own kind then. Balik India.'

'*Balik India?* Why should I? India is not my country. This is my country.'

We weren't screaming. We hissed loathing at each other.

'Pariah. Keling. Miserable black Indian. Always whining.'

'Entitled natives. Greedy, grasping, always wanting everything free of charge. Lazy. Shiftless.'

We stood facing each other, fangs bared. Unkind, contemptuous words. Where did they come from? I never ever dreamed we had caught them from the adults and kept them safe, nurtured in our bosoms.

Hsian tried to stop us. 'You're playing the same old rhetoric, both of you!' he cried. 'Change the game, you idiots. What's the matter with you?'

The matter was the serpent had escaped from where it was buried deep in our hearts and had emerged, hungry and angry. Auntie rushed out of her room. She told us to shut up and reached out to touch my arm. That was when I swatted her hand off and stormed away.

No one was home except Zul who looked at my face that felt all mottled and hot. He was alarmed. 'Are you crying? Did something happen? What did Arun do?'

I wasn't crying right up till that point but when he mentioned Arun, all the hurt and betrayal spilled over. 'I don't want to hear his name!' I went into my room and shut the door, ignoring Zul who banged on it, yelling, 'Did he hurt you? Did he hurt you? Farida?'

'Go away!'

* * *

Auntie has gone to the washroom. I've been waiting for her to go because something's been niggling at the back of my mind and I don't want her to hear it. 'Hsian, what happened really? All I know is you two were attacked at the basketball court in the playground last night.'

'No, I wasn't attacked, only him. I've told the police already.' His voice is flat and he keeps his eyes on Arun. 'We were messing around, shooting hoops. No one else was there. We weren't really in the mood—after the quarrel and all that. After you left, we were sitting around, crushed. Auntie was crying. Arun picked up the phone several times to call you. He was bitterly ashamed. He didn't know what to tell you but he called. You didn't answer.

'So, I was still messing around in the basketball court. Arun walked away and sat down in the bench near the gate. I was bouncing the ball when it flew off into the hedge. I went looking for it. Then I heard yelling and scuffling. I turned back and saw a boy beating Arun with a helmet. He must have hit him from the back first because Arun was on the ground, face down. He got up, unsteady, bleeding and he grappled with the boy. They rolled on the ground and the boy was howling and punching Arun. What chance did Arun have? That coward hit him on his head! Coward!' Hsian spits the word out. Hsian, shouting, ran towards them and the boy with one last kick at Arun, jumped on his motorbike and escaped.

I close my eyes. 'Did you recognize the boy?'

Hsian is silent. Then he says, 'Like I told the police, I was too far away.'

Something is not right. 'Why would he attack Arun? He didn't steal his wallet or his bag. What are you not telling me?' I grab his shirt. 'Was it someone you knew?'

'I've told you what I told the police and Auntie Ruku. It was a random attack. And when he wakes up, that's exactly what Arun will say too.'

A strange dread rises in me, rising from my stomach to clutch my throat. I can't breathe. I can't see. I want to throw up. 'Hsian?' I whisper.

'I won't say anything more, Farida. Arun won't either.' I hear the raggedness in his words. 'It stops with us, you see. It has to bloody well stop with us.'

Auntie comes back. Hsian and I are sitting next to Arun's bed. I'm curled up in my chair, one hand on my knees, the other, wrapped in Hsian's hand. Hsian's other arm rests on my shoulder. Auntie tut-tuts and says the stress has gotten to me. So, she sits by my side as well.

END

12

When I Speak of Kuala Lumpur

When I speak of Kuala Lumpur, I speak of the things you want to hear. Of the Twin Towers, like silver-tipped waves shimmering upon a moonless ocean. I've seen them up close from posh restaurants where my Mem takes the family for Sunday dinner.

The first time I mention the towers, you say, 'Girl, eating in posh restaurants? Ririn, I'm so happy for you!' The pride in your voice, Ma, it carries through the phone and cuts off my tongue so I can't say, *I don't eat* at those restaurants, Ma. I'm there to carry Mem's shopping bags. I watch as the family eats. I'm the servant, remember, and servants are invisible creatures. If I am invisible, how can my hunger exist?

I am a slave in my Mem's house, Ma. The bloody Indon, she calls me—she never calls me by my name. She hits me, and pinches me, digging her sharp nails into my skin, and jabs my head with her finger. If she catches her Ethan giving me a hug—I know I'll pay for it later. The kid senses it; he no longer comes near me when his mother is in the room. His grandma ignores me as well. They're kind that way.

When Mem first strikes me, I am so shocked that I insist on leaving immediately. Even Pa has never once hit me. Mem calls the maid agency and a man comes over, a small, slight man with glasses. He doesn't speak. He walks up to me, gives me a flying kick straight at my belly sending me sprawling to the floor. Then he pulls me up and slaps me. When he finally speaks, his words are without emotion. *One more word of complaint from your Mem and you can forget going back to Indonesia. I'll send you to work on the streets. Understand?* The pain in my belly winds itself all over my body. I cannot eat for two days. I don't know a single soul in this country. My Mem holds my passport, my future. *She owns me.*

Every night when I go to bed, sleep comes fragmented and with reluctance. So, I read my book of Pak Sapardi's poems and when even they fail me, I do what I always do, when the black fog shrouds me: I trace my journey back to our home. *Two hours in the bus from Jakarta airport, I get down at the bus stop in our village to run home. Pak Sugi's children paddle in the stream by their house; Ibu Karni's looking out the window. The wind from the rice fields brushes my face, the sun glows on my head; long shadows run, keeping pace with me and I smell the fragrance of home, long before I see it, as my feet hasten past Pak Ali giving his buffalo a wash. And there you are, Ma. Muna. Family. Home.*

You're laughing, Ma? Sentimental overkill—ya, I know. But I tell you: even if Mount Merapi covered our village with ash; even if our people, the earth, the trees, the flowers, the buffaloes were washed in only grey—even if, even if—our village would still be the most beautiful place on earth.

The end of the first month, after sending you my salary— thank you Western Union—I just want to return home. I call you, knowing you'd tell me to come back immediately. When I hear your voice, God, I almost burst into a great shudder of weeping but you cry out, 'Ririn, my darling, your money came just in time—Muna's gone to get us something to eat—' and the relief in your voice, it reaches out over the phone and cuts off my tongue.

So, when I speak to you, I speak of the things you want to hear; of this grand house without a garden, not a blade of grass or a flower or a tree; every inch of the grounds is cemented over. Nothing like our place, eh, Ma, where the trees fringe our house anyhow they like, and where, if I'm in the mood, I just go out and chop down a sugar cane and chomp on it, the sweet juices running down my throat.

I speak of meeting the other Indonesian maids when I take Ethan for a walk in the evenings. I tell you about speaking Javanese for the first time since coming to Malaysia and how I feel almost high as the words roll on my tongue like remembered music—I could have danced that day, right on the road.

I don't tell you that the maid next door, Ningsih, has given me telephone numbers of places to go to if I ever run away. Ningsih's like a sleek cat, smug in the way kind people are whose dreams have all come true—but she's got her finger on the pulse of things. Mem's previous maid ran away two days before I arrived, she says. I'm the emergency replacement. And Mem's husband, he's left her. He's fighting her in the courts for Ethan. She's not letting him near the child.

I do tell you that Ningsih is among the lucky ones. She's been with the same family for over twenty years. I tell you she's paid almost eleven million rupiah a month and you say you can't believe it. Ningsih gets to go home to Jogja for a month every year. Her employers pay for her tickets, her shopping—everything. *I can't stay away for more than a month*, she laughs. *The house falls apart without me.* I also say, 'Ma, she asks if my family is saving up part of my salary for me.' You are quiet for so long I think we've been cut off. Then you say, 'Yes, yes, of course I shall do it. I have your bank book, don't worry.' I don't worry. Muna comes on the line and I forget all about the savings.

When I speak of Kuala Lumpur to Muna—oh how I love to hear her voice, Ma—she's such a giddy goat—she babbles on about the new clothes you buy her, her new bag, the smartphone. 'Have you got a smartphone, Ririn?'

'No.'

'You can take photos and send them to us, you know. Why don't you get one?'

'Because I send all my money home.'

'Oh.'

'Are you studying hard, Muna?'

'Yes, relax, Ririn.' You take the phone from her. You don't mention the smartphone.

* * *

My Mem—I don't think she's ever played with her son. That's my job. She takes him and grandma out for a meal on weekends. That's hers. Grandma's job—she doesn't have any.

Grandma watches Chinese and Korean serials all day. She talks to me of a time when her daughter was younger, when she wasn't such a piece of work. I tell her that her daughter's selective about her victims. She pretends not to hear. 'I dunno what to do, lah. Very tiring.'

'Don't see, don't hear, Grandma!' I wave my hands and smile. She looks sheepish and returns to her serials. In the afternoons, when I have a bit of time, I massage her legs. She likes that. She's a sort of friend; the sort that slips me a chocolate or even ten bucks when no one's watching; the sort that also disappears when her daughter hits me. I speak English pretty well by the way, for this family, they speak in no other language, not even Chinese. Can you imagine? *I speak English, Ma.* Ethan, all of five years old, is teaching me to read it. We're on fairy tales now.

When I speak to Muna, I tell her what I've learned, 'Once upon a time, Muna . . . once upon a time, they lived happily ever after.' She teases me that I'm becoming an Englishwoman. We laugh together though I do sense a creeping annoyance in her. 'Ririn, you're *sooo* clever, first poetry, and now English.' I tell her to work hard in school and she dismisses me, 'Yeah, yeah, stop fussing. You always liked school better than me.'

I last eight months in that house. The night before I run away, I'm on the phone with you. I love to hear your voice, Ma, you know that? You're my heart's anchor. We talk and then you say almost as an apology, 'Your father's come back.'

I'm punched in the stomach. 'No-no-no-no-no! You promised me, Ma, you promised, you wouldn't let him back again.'

'Ririn, he's worried about me and Muna. That we're all alone.'

'Oh yeah? Since when?' I ask and then I know at once why my father's home. 'You told him I was in Kuala Lumpur, and sending money home to you, didn't you? Didn't you, Ma?' I was snarling at you, remember? 'Has he asked you for money yet?'

Your voice turns into ice. 'He's your father. Treat him with respect.' You hang up. For the first time, Ma, you actually hang up on me. I'm losing you over Pa; over a man who left us for another woman, and never ever asked how we were managing. I can't believe it. My heart is bursting. I don't know what to do. I can't sit or stand and then when my Mem comes home and shoves me against the kitchen wall, I snap at her. 'Stop it!' All at once, she's howling, pulping me, pulling my hair and kicking me. This rage is different and I'm terrified. I yell at the top of my lungs, 'Police! Police!' Grandma comes running from her room and pushes Mem away. 'Die—die! You want to go to prison-ah? You want?'

Mem is shaking. 'That bloody Indon—' They scream at each other. Ethan wakes up wailing and comes down the stairs. Mem stomps off to her room. I'm lying crumpled on the floor. It feels like all my bones are smashed and the pain is unbearable. Grandma quietens Ethan down and settles him in bed. She takes a long time before she comes to me. I'm sitting in my room, my head in my hands. She nudges me. I look up. She has two painkillers in her hand and a glass of water. She gives them to me. I say: 'I don't care anymore. I'm calling the police.' Grandma shakes her head. 'I can't protect you, Ririn, but I can do this.' She gives me something. My passport. 'I took it from the drawer in her study,' she says.

I look at her. 'I don't have any money'.

The next morning, Mem drives off to work. Ethan is playing with his toys; his grandma's watching a Korean serial. I tell them I am going out. Grandma smiles at me sadly and I drop a kiss on Ethan's head. My passport's in my pocket with Grandma's old smartphone that she was going to give to Ethan to play with. It's a bribe, along with two months' salary so that I don't go to the police. I know where to go. I have the contacts.

* * *

Remember how it all started, Ma? The stranger who came to our village? He didn't say, 'If you work as a maid in Malaysia, you will be able to buy ten houses and ten hectares of land.' Hah! Who'd have believed that? Instead, he said, 'You will get six million rupiah a month.'

Six million. You and I, we'd never ever seen six million rupiah in our lives.

'If you go with him, Ririn,' you say, 'Muna can go to college and become—what is it you want her to become?'

Teacher. Anything. So long as she doesn't get married at fifteen like her mother and sister. 'Will you do that, Muna? Do you promise to study? And not listen to our father and get married next year?' My sister nods, her face solemn. I have dreams for Muna. They don't include being forced to leave school at fourteen, getting a husband at fifteen and getting divorced at seventeen like myself. They don't include a waste-of-space like our father. You know how much I begged him, don't you Ma? I wanted to study, not get married. What did he say? 'You want to become a poet? Fool!'

You and me, Ma, we make barely enough, peddling bottles of jamu in the morning market in town. Some days, if we sell extra bottles, I put money into my savings account and drop by the second-hand bookshop near the bank to browse the books.

Every time the bookseller sees me, he lends me a book or two, free of charge. I think he's sweet on me.

Pa—he doesn't work. Chasing a new woman, setting the world to rights in the coffeeshop or gambling on fighting cocks takes up all his time.

'Ma, if I leave, I don't want Pa to come back to our house and live off my money.'

'Not likely,' you say but your face is sad. 'He's happy where he is. He's married another girl, I hear. Why would he want to come back?' I should have seen it then. Some women need their husbands the way I need my poetry. Me, my belly remains taut after two years of marriage with not even a worm in my womb. When my husband divorces me, neither of us sheds great tears. Still, as a parting shot, he tells me, 'Goodbye ugly.' Strange how the most unimportant people can pierce you right through. I carry that wound like an open sore in my heart for years until a Bangla man, handsome, desire in his eyes, tells me shyly, 'You're beautiful, Ririn.'

I travel to the airport in Jakarta in the stranger's sleek Mercedes. Everyone in the village comes out to wave goodbye. I sit in the back of the car while the stranger—*call me Pak Harto*—in his fine cotton batik shirt and leather shoes sits in front with the driver. I have a brand-new passport. I already feel like six million rupiah.

He'd lied of course. Everything is a lie. The salary is three million rupiah, not six million. The agent who meets me at the airport in Malaysia, takes away my passport. I have no documents, nothing. I've flown into a strange country on easy lies, straight into the great underbelly of illegals in Malaysia.

* * *

I speak to you a week after I leave Mem's house. You are frantic. 'You can't send any money this month?'

'It's going to be hard for a while, Ma . . . '

'I'm sure she didn't mean to be nasty to you, Ririn.'

'Ma, she beat me so hard she could have killed me.'

You're not listening. You fret. 'I don't know what your father is going to say. Listen darling—you think she'll take you back, if you go to her and say you're sorry?'

You cut off my tongue, Ma. You splinter my insides. I don't call you for two weeks. You don't call me either.

* * *

Indon Flats. That's what the locals call the place where I stay. A low-rise block hidden among other flats and terrace houses, it's barely a kilometre from the newest, most happening shopping mall. Most are our people, though there are a few Banglas crowded into three flats. I know one of them. Rahman. He works at a petrol station, putting in twelve hours a day. He smiles at me and calls me 'beautiful'. I wonder how it'll be to have a man touch me, kiss me, caress me again . . . I feel light-headed just thinking about it.

One local chap stays on the first floor with his family. He's a minor politician with long arms into many government departments. He's like our headman, collecting our rents and paying off the authorities so they don't raid us. 'Cos almost everyone is an illegal, see.

Let's play a quick game Ma. Come on, it's fun. No, don't yell. It's called *Ask Me a Question.* Here goes. Question One: *If you are an illegal and you want to blend in like a local, what must you do?* The clock's running, be quick, Ma. You don't know the answer? Hah. It's simple. *Wear a hijab and keep your mouth shut!* Keep your mouth shut, you get it, Ma? Because our accent gives us away! Hahaha! Question Two: *If you are an illegal and you want to keep your money safe from the uniforms when you go out, what do you do?*

I'll answer that—it isn't fair to ask you. *You hide the money 1) inside your hijab 2) inside your socks 3) inside hidden pockets in your panties.*

*You make sure you tuck a fifty ringgit note in your purse so that if you don't
run away fast enough, that money is your ticket to freedom.*

When I speak to you next, I tell you I'm already cleaning
several houses a week. You're relieved. We don't mention our
previous conversation. I speak of my flat that I share with two
other women, Mirna and Tini, both illegals. They work in a
Chinese restaurant. I tell you they've been in Malaysia for years.
I don't tell you that quickly enough, I realize they're lovers. How,
you might ask. I'll tell you: the way Tini slides her hand around
Mirna's waist with such tenderness that I almost weep for no
one has ever touched me that way. Or when they're sitting on
the sofa with Tini's feet on Mirna's lap. They're doing nothing,
you understand, they're not even talking, but that intimacy—I feel
it like a sunburst inside me. There was a time I would've been
disgusted at such things between woman and woman, Ma, except
now that there's been no loving in my life for so long, I'm gentler
with my thoughts. I don't know how kind you'll be, so I cut off
my own tongue.

I don't have time now to tell you about my employers, but
I learned this: on the billboards along the streets, they show
everybody being best friends with each other but the Chinese,
Indians, Malays, they live in their own bubbles and the politicians
make sure they don't trust each other too much. Still, they all
have one thing in common—they despise us. All of us invisible
creatures that live below the surface—from Indonesia, Bangladesh,
Myanmar, Cambodia, India, Vietnam, Philippines. They despise
us but who else will clean their homes or collect their garbage
or build their houses? It's funny you know, when you think the
Chinese and Indians were once immigrants themselves? Ha. You
think they'd be kind to us. Ha. Ha. Ha. I try to explain this to
Muna because she's in school and surely, she'll find it interesting.
She says, 'Ala, Ririn, so boring, like a history lesson!'

Mirna knows it all. 'In this country, all the chest-thumping
about race and religion is just that—empty sounds. In the end,

only money counts, Ririn. And someone to blame when things go wrong.' Mirna and Tini, they send money home to their husbands and children whom they love. In Malaysia, they love each other. I say I send money home as well and my mother's saving up for me. Aren't you, Ma?

I ask them, 'However will you get home? Your passports are expired already.' They shrug. *Any number of ways.* I realize I have much to learn.

Like how to pay attention. Remember I tell you this and I laugh till I get the hiccups. I'm with Tini, waiting at the bus stop near our flat. I look around and smile at the whole waiting bunch, mostly Indonesians and Banglas. The bus is due any minute now when a boy on a bike races towards us. *Polisi!* he yells. In five seconds flat, the bus stop is empty—except for me, still smiling, still waiting. Tini dashes back and grabs my hand, shouting, *Run! Police!* We run all the way to our flat. Telling you this, I laugh but you cry at my narrow escape, and once again, you're my anchor, the way you've always been.

Don't hang up on me just yet, Ma, I'm coming to the important bit now. You promised me ten minutes. Remember, you call me and you speak with that soft pleading I know so well. 'The roof is leaking, Ririn. Muna keeps falling sick.' Muna. My baby sister. All night I can't sleep. I imagine her delirious, wracked with fever, lying in a damp room with rain dribbling down through the ceiling. The money you ask for is beyond me though you insist you need it within the week. The next few days, Ma, I work like a demented woman. I beg my employers to give me more hours and more. I work for their neighbours and friends. Shameless, I borrow money from Tini and Mirna, money they can't afford to give. All week, I eat only hot rice with soy sauce and a green chilli to save more money. I send you whatever I get.

When I call you a few days later, Muna answers and Ma, she's whooping and laughing and she tells me, 'Ri Riiiin! We have the biggest television ever in the entire village, no, in the entire universe!'

'Hang on, Muna, I don't understand. What about the leaky roof?'

'What leaky roof?

'And how are you feeling?'

'Dunno. All right I guess.'

'Where's Ma?'

She gives the phone to you. At first, I can't understand what you say; your words trip over each other. They race into the phone like a rooster chasing a chicken. *Your father got this fantastic offer it was a special price because your father is his friend your father knows everyone bless him he said don't let go this offer you'll never get it again imagine such a fine television full colour no one in the village has one like it your father is so clever we're so happy the house is full of people everyone comes to see us and watch shows on our television I am so happy please be happy for us Ririn. And yes, it's stopped raining so we can wait to repair the roof when you next send us the money.*

I sink to the floor. I'm shaking so much that I sound incoherent even to my own ears. I don't realize even as my blouse is stained wet that I'm howling. When I do realize it, I can't control it. I can bear pain, Ma, you know that, but this grief, it's so raw it swallows me whole and I'm drowning, and I can't breathe. I can't remember what I say; only your words are seared in my brain. *Why can't you be happy for us? You can't bear for us to be happy, can you? So what if you ate only rice and soy sauce for a week? We never asked you to. Stop trying to make us feel bad.* On and on and on. *We were so happy and now you've spoiled everything. It's just a bloody TV, Ririn.*

I hear knocking on the door. You haven't stopped talking and I can't put the phone down, Ma. It's stuck to my hand. I stumble to the door, open it. Mirna and Tini are standing there. I'm sobbing so loudly their eyes go wide open and I fall into their arms.

Mirna and Tini leave for their evening shift at the Chinese restaurant. I take a shower. I am suddenly ravenous for chicken biryani. Can you believe that, Ma? One week of white rice with soy sauce and a green chilli and now I want biryani from the mamak restaurant next to where my friends work.

The restaurant owner knows me. I sometimes help out when he's especially busy during festivals. I'm about to tuck in when just like in the movies, there's a huge commotion outside. Police cars and trucks. The uniforms spill out and race to the Chinese restaurant. I know I should run and hide but my legs can't move. I'm frozen to my seat. The restaurant owner places his songkok on his head, goes to the entrance and waits, watchful. His illegal workers have all melted away. Later, he tells whoever is listening, 'That Chinese boss didn't pay enough money to the uniforms, that's all there is to it.'

I pretend to eat. Each grain of rice feels like sand on my tongue. For not the first time, it hits me that I'm in a country that doesn't like me. An old Malay couple, the man wearing a white skullcap and his wife in a flowery hijab, bring their plates of rice over to my table and sit down. The old man nods at me. 'Eat, child,' he says. 'If anyone asks, you're our daughter.' Such kindness. I cry and the woman pats my hand.

The raid is over quickly. I raise my head and see the restaurant workers being led away to a truck and driven off. One Vietnamese cook, two Bangla workers. My Tini and Mirna.

I sit up deep into the night, seeking solace, any solace from Pak Sapardi's poems.

'Nothing is more enduring
than the rain in June
hiding its yearning
for the tree in bloom'

* * *

Pak Sapardi speaks of me, Ma; he speaks to me. I wonder what will happen to Tini and Mirna after they're deported. Will they manage to come back? I think they will. I think about you and me, Ma; about how you are always a wife more than you are ever a mother. It's not something that's right or wrong. It just is. Pa is first priority with you; you will always put him first over us. Who am I to say it's wrong? Tini's words earlier in the evening come to me: 'A bit hard, ya, for them to be constantly grateful to you, Ririn. Don't grudge them a bit of luxury.'

'I starved for them,' I say, my voice swollen with weeping. 'I worked like a dog to get money for the damned roof.' I feel your betrayal stab me in my heart once again. Mirna shakes her head. 'Ririn, we're all different. Some of us are born to carry our family's burdens. Others—' she shrugs. 'They just live off us.'

'I wish I could go back. Everything was fine when I was there and my father wasn't.'

Tini's voice is sad. 'You can never go back, Ririn. Nothing's the same as before. Not you. Not even your house.'

When I call you next, I say I'm sorry for shouting at you. You cry a little. I ask where's Muna and you say, 'Remember Pak Harto? The man who hired you?' Your voice rings with suppressed excitement. 'He says he's got a job for Muna in Malaysia. A nice family, he says—they'll treat her like a daughter and not a maid.'

'Ma, what are you saying? She's just fifteen.'

'I know, but Pak Harto—he's ever so kind—he says he can change her birthdate so she's eighteen instead of fifteen. Your father says—'

'Are you crazy?' My fear jumps out from my throat. I cannot control it. 'She's going to be a teacher!'

'That's your dream for her, Ririn, not hers. She's not interested in studying.' You are gentle with pity.

'Ma, listen, she cannot c-come here.' My voice is shaking so badly that my words are crushed before they come out.

'They'll t-treat her like a s-slave. Th-they'll beat her and sh-sh-she w-w-won't know wh-wh-what to do.'

You hear what you want to hear. 'You don't want your sister to work in Malaysia? To eat in posh restaurants? To earn better than what a teacher can earn here?' You sound incredulous.

I can't believe this is happening. I swallow hard. 'Dear God. Ma, let me speak with her.'

You tell me she's gone with Pak Harto to apply for a passport. She'll leave as soon as she gets it. I beg you; I beg you to listen to me for ten minutes without interrupting. You raise your voice. You say I can't change your mind. I say 'Give me the ten minutes, Ma, please. You owe me that at least.' Then I start:

When I speak of Kuala Lumpur, I speak of the things you want to hear. Of the Twin Towers, like silver-tipped waves shimmering upon a moonless ocean. I've seen them up close from posh restaurants where my Mem takes the family for Sunday dinner . . .

You cry. 'That's the life I want for my Muna, you selfish idiot!'

I don't eat at those restaurants, Ma. I'm there to carry Mem's shopping bags. I watch as the family eats. I'm the servant, remember, and servants are invisible creatures. If I am invisible, how can my hunger exist?

Even as I speak, you keep yelling. 'Shut up! Shut up, you liar! Liar!'

I know then that you will surely send Muna to Malaysia, whatever I say. Still, I don't let you get a word in though you try. I have a ten-minute window and I intend to speak for all of it.

I am a slave in my Mem's house, Ma. The bloody Indon, she calls me— she never calls me by my name. She hits me, and pinches me, digging her sharp nails into my skin, and jabs my head with her finger . . .

END

---

*From Sapardi Djoko Damono's *Hujan Bulan Juni* published by Gramedia Pustaka Utama, 1994. Translated with permission.

13

Cartwheels on the Corridor

My mother and I went back to Melati Flats to say a last goodbye to my home. We walked not together, not touching, not talking, not sharing, for that was what we had become.

When it was built in 1970, a decade before I was born, the four-storey walk-up was a showcase of optimistic housing for the working class in Kuala Lumpur. Last painted when it was newly built, Melati Flats was now resolute in its decline. It distrusted all authority except Shankar's father, because no one was inclined to oppose him. It particularly mistrusted the police. Even Azam's father, a sacked policeman, was allowed to stay only because of his wife's nasi lemak. She had a makeshift stall at the entrance to the flats and there was always a queue at breakfast. In later years, Azam's father's friend, a policeman, as mean as Azam's father, took to coming over for free breakfast at the stall.

My mother had sold the flat. We were strangers to it already. We were leaving all furnishings, taking nothing except what my mother wanted now, some bits from here and there. Already the flat wore a sheen of decay, a whiff of mouldy uncleanliness. I sensed the ghosts that lurked in the darkened rooms, sulky, deprived of human company, shadowing our steps. It was a good thing I wasn't afraid of ghosts. Since Shankar was gone, I'd been afraid of nothing.

The familiar faces in the flats on that second floor were gone too although it was said Shankar's father had returned. My mother seemed wary of meeting him, with good reason. Azam was holed up in his Polytech; he refused to respond to my calls or emails. His mother gave up her nasi lemak business and went back to her kampong; she'd threatened Azam's father with physical assault by all her relatives if he ever showed his face there. The man disappeared one day. Just like that.

My mother stopped to visit a friend on the ground floor so I walked alone through our once home in silence, saying goodbye to the impossibly tiny bedrooms, the kitchen which was always dark, the living room where curtains from Globe Silk Store still hung proudly; where a brand new colour television had held pride of place. My father had bought the TV when I was three years old. I remember him beaming as the neighbours crowded in every evening to watch the shows in colour. We were only the second family in the flats to own a colour TV; Shankar's of course, was the first.

It was to this living room that Shankar's father carried me as gently as if I were a baby when I was seven. Bruised, tears streaking down my face, my dress torn, my panties missing, my eyes unseeing, I remember Shankar sobbing, his hand clutching mine. *Even then, it had been Shankar who'd saved me.* I remember Shankar's father handing me carefully into my father's arms, my mother's shrieks that rang loud as temple bells. I don't remember what he told them but Shankar's father stopped my mother and father from doing murder that day.

I do remember whispers about a boy, the sundry shop assistant who was severely beaten up later that night by thugs who smashed his right hand. Instead of filing a police report, the boy disappeared from his hospital bed. I can't remember his face or his name but the image of that hand snaking towards me and then grabbing me by my arm, hitting me when I began to whimper, ripping off my panties, shoving me to the floor, and filling my body with near total paralysis, has never left me.

Standing in the living room, the memory of that day broke away from its dam and I found myself stamping on his faceless face again and again, stamping it into the ground.

I was so proud of myself, wasn't I, going to the shop all by myself like a grown-up. I held the coins in my hand carefully. Fifty cents for scrapped coconut, for my mother to make candy. The shop, usually open seven days a week, appeared closed, but the collapsible grill gate wasn't completely shut and when I peered in, someone pulled me inside and I screamed. When I wouldn't stop screaming, a hand covered my mouth hard. Shankar, walking home from a hawker stall with his father, heard my voice. They couldn't find me anywhere at first. Shankar kept calling me. He must have sensed movement inside the store for his father pushed the gate aside, kicked open the door and found us.

Many years later, Shankar told me that I needed therapy to talk it all out. We never talked about it, my parents and I. Afterwards, my mother bathed me, scrubbing the taint from my body. My father hugged me and they both cried and they put me to bed and that was that. *The shame! The shame! What will people say? What will happen to our family honour?* Those were unspoken fears so real that we pretended what had happened had never happened.

* * *

It was said my mother tried the deception when she first held me. She wore a batik kaftan with purple and green motifs, which she had bought from the Indian Muslim shop down the road, to be paid for at three dollars a month for six months. She had oiled her frizz into submission and drawn it into a bun. Her red pottu, the size of a ten-cent coin sat in the middle of her forehead. She waited in her living room, smiling, hiding her annoyance that the women, *all of them*, from *all* the neighbouring flats had decided to drop by just at that time. She had no idea that a buzz had gone around that Saroja was getting a baby.

As my father laid me in her arms, a golden-skinned baby with stiff hair, slanted eyes, fat cheeks, my mother kissed me, crooning, 'My baby from my womb, *my* womb!' She turned to the women. 'She came two weeks early. Her father had to rush me to hospital.' The women looked back at her. 'Almost twelve at night, it was.' Her voice rose, defiant. 'He had to take me on his motorbike, didn't he? Couldn't get a taxi.' She sighed. 'I was perched on the Honda, holding my stomach with one hand, holding his waist with the other.'

'Then you came home early without the baby?'

'What? Oh. She had a bit of fever. Had to stay back.'

'Yeah, right,' muttered someone. 'Saroja, every day I see you and every day, you're not pregnant but now you say you've given birth!' she snorted. 'And the baby doesn't even look Indian . . . No shame saying you adopted a baby, you know.'

'Eh?' my mother sparkled outrage. 'Who said that? Who dares to say it—to my face? I gave birth to her, what? I swear! Stupid me!' Here, she hit her forehead. 'Should have taken out an ad, right, saying, *Hey, I'm pregnant* . . . ' She would have gone on except that my father, exasperated for once, told her, '*Summa iru pulle.*' Give it a rest, girl. It was my first encounter, though I did not know it, of storytellers and the shifting of truth in the real world.

My mother's truth was elastic. She never acknowledged my ethnicity. My skin was Chinese; my hair was straight without a single Indian curl; my eyes were Chinese. Only my nose, thanks to her constant massaging when I was a baby, was shapely and high. 'Have I told you that my grandfather was exceptionally fair?' she told people. 'Janaki's colouring is all his.'

Summa iru pulle, my father would say, his smile taking the sting away from his words.

The other elephant in the room that she ignored was that time when I was molested. *Shankar's father saved me we never talked about it I mostly forgot about it unless something triggered the memory and released the horror and the fear that seized my throat making me almost mute, almost catatonic.* She never talked about it. Neither did my father.

* * *

My mother came into the flat. She didn't notice my pallor or that I was gripping the edge of a chair. 'This room,' she said, her hand sweeping over the living room, 'it has held all our best stories. It was here that I carried you for the first time . . . ' she paused, 'and held you in my heart forever after that.' She said it softly almost to herself. In that moment, I saw what she saw, a mother who loved her daughter with all her heart. I also saw more but I kept it to myself. We had already hurt each other beyond reconciliation. I didn't need to tell her that from the beginning, her love for me had stifled all the magic in life, all fun, all adventure. In her world, a good daughter was one who listened and submitted without question. I was a major failure in both categories.

'You don't love me though,' she remarked. 'Is it because your Chinese blood can't love an Indian mother?'

I laughed, clenching my fists until my nails dug into my palms. Here was someone who had bought a Chinese child and then proceeded to make the child as Indian as possible but from the time I was thirteen, she had pressed all the necessary buttons to make sure I never forgot I was Chinese. I went for the kill. 'Why did you hate Shankar so much?'

She didn't expect the question. She flinched. She walked away, muttering something about checking if she still wanted some bowls and plates from the kitchen. I let her be. I heard her banging the cabinet doors in the kitchen. I wanted nothing from my home except an exercise book where my father had laboriously pasted Calvin and Hobbes strips, collected from newspapers discarded by patients in the hospital he worked. It was already safe in my bag.

One more person, apart from my mother, hated Shankar and his father. Azam's father. We didn't know it then. Ironically, my mother and he got on pretty well. She'd pass him hot Indian curries and sweet desserts; he'd pass her his wife's nasi lemak. They were two parents united by the utter disappointment in their children. Azam was laid back, gentle, easily happy; scarcely competitive. I—I was a hellcat who'd do cartwheels in the living room, and down the corridor outside the flat, accepting my punishment without a sound.

When did Azam's father begin to hate Shankar and his father? That day when Azam got his head repeatedly knuckled for buying sweets and sharing them with Shankar and me outside his flat. It was his sixth birthday and his mother had given him money to get himself a treat. 'Millionaire's son, izzit, to give your friends your sweets?' Azam's father knuckle-knocked him on the head. 'Your Chinese and Indian friends lining up to give you things izzit, fool?' Another hard knuckle on the head again. I surreptitiously slid my sweets into my pocket. I wasn't about to give them back. They were my favourite caramels.

'Please stop it!' Shankar said, crying. 'Here, take back the sweets. Don't hit him!' He clung on to Azam's father's arm and wouldn't let go even as the man tried to shrug him off.

Azam's mother rushed out of the house. 'It's his birthday today! Don't hit my son!'

'I'll hit him all I like,' he said, pushing her aside and that was when Shankar's father, coming out from his flat to see what the commotion was, picked him up by his collar as if he weighed nothing. 'Hit your son again and I will hit you right back.' Shankar's father was wearing a thin cotton vest; his forearms bulged with tattoos. Azam's father was a weaselly man, small-sized, more used to being snarky than anything else. He didn't hit his son again.

* * *

When I was little, skin colour was something invisible to my eyes. It didn't exist. It didn't exist when I was in Standard One; it still didn't exist in Standard Two. When I was nine and in Standard Three, my mother came to school on Report Card Day.

For the first time, I saw her through the eyes of my giggling classmates and ran to hide from this dark, fat woman, her face covered with beads of sweat that she wiped with a corner of her saree. It was a fair walk from the bus stop to our school.

Aiyoh, Janaki, your mother-ah? Why so black one!

So fat!

Why she and you so different?

She looked around for me but I was hiding and she couldn't find me and I could see the bewilderment in her eyes. Shankar, who was in Standard Four, found me. 'Why are you hiding, idiot? Your Amma's here. Come!' Pulling me along, Shankar ran to my mother and tucked his hand in hers as if it was the most natural thing in the world. A brief resistance from her hand before she clasped his.

Growing up inseparable, always running in and out of each other's homes, playing on the corridor together, Shankar, Azam and I—we could have been poster kids to celebrate a diverse Malaysia. Only, diversity wasn't celebrated except during elections.

* * *

I was thirteen when my mother finally stopped passing off her grandfather's genes as mine. A new neighbour dropped by to visit my mother. I made coffee and took it out to them. I was in shorts and a T-shirt. I was proud of my hair, newly bobbed in spite of my mother who wanted me in long plaits. The neighbour took one look at me and said, 'Chinese ah? Your daughter Chinese ah?'

Before she could reply, I said, 'Jeez, what gave me away? My skin colour? My eyes?'

She studied me with all seriousness and said, 'Yeah, the eyes are so Chinese and also you look Chinese . . . I knew straightaway, cannot fool me.'

I collapsed on the sofa and started laughing. The next thing I knew, my mother had plonked herself next to me and we put our arms around each other and laughed till tears slid down our cheeks. My mother never tried that deceit again.

* * *

Even as children, we recognized a hierarchy of our fathers in Melati Flats. My father, as a hospital worker *who would get a government pension* when he retired, ensuring life-long stability, was high up above pavement vendors, restaurant helpers, vegetable sellers. He was much higher than Azam's father who got sacked as a police constable—caught red-handed, they said though doing what, we never knew—and was subsequently chronically unemployed.

At the crown of the father hierarchy was of course Shankar's father, hands down, because he sold videos and therefore Shankar always had the latest cartoons that we could watch on his VCR. None of us could match that.

We didn't know until we were much older that Shankar's father made and sold pirated videos and that it was a crime. We didn't know that he had gangland connections. Our adults didn't tell us he'd been to prison.

The first we knew about Shankar's father was thanks to Azam's father when Shankar was in Standard One. We were at Azam's house, making too much noise disturbing the man when he was trying to take a nap. 'Oi, quiet, you gangster's son!' he yelled. 'You think what, just because your father is a gangster you can come here and bully my kid?'

The flat erupted with noise; everybody started talking at once. 'Gangster? What's a gangster?' Shankar.

'He's not bullying me, Ayah, we're not fighting . . . ' Azam. 'I get more marks in Malay than him . . . '

'Shut up, stupid fella. And why are you and that silly fool—' nodding at me '—following him around and listening to him? He's your king, izzit?'

'I'm not a silly fool, don't call me silly. I'm better in English than your son or Shankar, I even got a prize.'

'This whole block is safe and peaceful because of Shankar's father. What have you done to make it safe, huh? Sitting here, doing nothing, can't even get a job but talking big, very big.' This, from Azam's mother, waving her hands which smelled heavenly from the pandan and serai she was smashing for her nasi lemak.

'I SAID SHUT UP YOU FOOLS!' Azam's father grabbed something to throw at us but we were faster. We ran out of the flat before that thing hit the door.

'Cool, Shankar,' Azam said when we had caught our breath. 'Is your father really a gangster?'

'I don't know, I'll ask,' Shankar said, his eyes shining.

There was a story, probably made up by some wise cracking adult, that did the rounds when we were small. We heard it but could never fathom it. Shankar's father's name was Maniam. *One day some stranger came to Melati Flats to see Mr Maniam. 'Which Maniam do you want,' he was asked. 'Beer Maniam, Teacher Maniam, Romantic Maniam or Suicide Maniam?' 'I'm looking for the man who sells videos.' 'Oh, you mean Gangster Maniam.'* I was sixteen when I came across a similar joke with Irish names in an English magazine.

* * *

It was whispered that Shankar's mother died of an overdose when he was a baby and that was why his father never dealt in drugs. Shankar grew up without a mum so he was always looking to mine. As a child, he was always hugging her though she pushed him away. Azam's mother would have made a warmer substitute so I could never understand why it was mine that he wanted. He craved her approval.

She raged that Shankar and I were almost inseparable—'It's unnatural,' she kept saying. 'They're too close, always together, things can happen.' My father said, 'You can't see it? Nothing will happen. He's not made for girls.'

'Nonsense,' she told him.

I didn't know what he was talking about. My father liked Shankar and agreed to look after him if ever his father had to leave town on business. My mother though, found the going tough. Shankar was almost constantly in our flat for months at a time, stretching my mother's sanity to breaking point. That unbearable day, Shankar and I were laughing together at some stupid joke when he cried, 'My father will love this.'

'Well, you'll have to wait a few months to tell him, won't you, seeing he's in prison and all that,' my mother said almost immediately,

That image is imprinted in my mind: Shankar's animal cry *Amma*! His crumbling face as he put the jigsaw parts together; the blood draining from his face; and from my mother, grim-eyed unyielding refusal to back down. Somewhere in the background, my father was shouting at my mother even as I moved to hug Shankar from behind and hold him.

My father yelled: *Wunakku thaanga mudiyile, pulle! Yaen intha veri?* No, Appa, I could have told him. She couldn't bear it. You can't control manic hatred. Or the fear that Shankar and I were too close, maybe even falling in love. I thought it was ridiculous of course—I was fourteen, for heaven's sake. It took me years to understand that in her world, a young man was either a brother or a husband. He couldn't be a best friend to a girl.

* * *

I hated my mother. I hated that Shankar stopped coming over to our flat. We'd long forgotten the 'gangster' bit about Shankar's father. We accepted that he sold videos at night markets in the various towns nearby. We accepted that he called Shankar once a week on the phone and said that everything was fine with him. We never wondered, never questioned. We were stupid and it was not a pleasant realization to find out the truth of it. Stupid, dumb bloody innocents as my mother could have described it if she'd wanted.

We were not in love, Shankar and I. There was nothing sweetly romantic about what I felt for him. He was my friend in a way that the word 'friend' couldn't adequately cover. I woke up happy in the morning because I'd be seeing him. Even when we quarrelled as kids and fought to kill—l did, not him—there was always that knowing that we were friends forever and me bashing him wouldn't change a thing. He was necessary to me in that same steadfast knowledge I had that I'd wobble from fatigue if I didn't rest or die if I didn't eat or stop living if I didn't breathe. It didn't matter to him or me, that he liked boys. I sensed it but my father recognized it. Only my mother rejected it outright. I could have told her that when I was with Shankar or thought of him, there was this feeling in my heart that everything was in its right place in my world but she would not have understood the truth of it.

I couldn't spell it out then the way I can now but I knew instinctively that there were many kinds of loving despite what adults said. Years later, I knew that if Shankar had suggested making love, I would have gleefully, teasingly embraced him.

We would have laughed and tickled each other. We would have made love. And I would still have been his best friend. It was as uncomplicated as that.

* * *

When my father retired, he discovered his pension was miniscule—'won't even buy face powder for your mother', a dig at my mother's love for the *Three Beauties* pressed face powder. He got a job as a security guard in a factory and about the same time, my mother was hired as a cook in a charity home within walking distance. 'And I got the job, Mister *Hate Compact Powder*, thanks to the smooth glowing beauty of my complexion, see?'

'Yeah, right,' my father grinned. '*Summa iru pulle!*'

After his release, Shankar's father moved to a different part of town, working as a nightclub bouncer. Sometimes I saw him in Shankar's flat and the way they held each other, heads burrowed into each other's hair, made me shush with pain. 'When I first saw him, I wanted to hit him,' Shankar told me. 'But when he realized that I'd found out about him being in prison, he just shrivelled.' As if all the stories he'd told Shankar had come to bind him up in ropes he couldn't unravel. Prison had made his father ragged with fear. He spoke of a different world now with drugs and guns as currency and not just in the underworld; this was a world where even the police had changed. He knew of angry murmurs on the ground about Indian men picked up for questioning and found dead in police custody. Brutality. Torture. Murder, the whispers said. The newspapers said death was due to natural causes. Sometimes they mentioned stomach ulcers.

'Get away from here, son. Go far away as possible. Because it's only a matter of time for me. They'll come for me sooner or later,' he said.

'They?' Shankar asked. 'Who's the they? They're already here, Appa. All the gangs already know who I am. You know how many times I'm pressed to join this gang or that? Almost daily. Because I am your son. I can't escape them, anywhere I turn. Even if I move to another town.'

'You have to get away from this country, son.'

Australia. That's where Shankar planned to go. He was an apprentice with an electrician and doing an evening course in a vocational college. He was studying to get professional certification.

He could earn a decent income in Australia as a licensed electrician. The country needed a whole lot of skilled people, he heard. Would I go to Australia too, he asked me. 'We'll ask Azam as well.' I had no money, no qualifications yet.

'Of course,' I told him. I had completed my sixth form exams and begun work as a temporary teacher in a private school while waiting for my results. I planned to save money and apply for a nursing degree. Surely, Australia needed nurses. 'I'll go first and you can follow once you finish your degree,' he said. 'Melbourne. We'll go to Melbourne.'

I told my father about it. My mother went ballistic when she overheard it. 'You're not doing nursing. You're not going to Australia. He's not taking you away from me.'

At times like this, I wondered once again about the Chinese mother who had sold me. What had she been thinking? Had she cared? Had she cried? Had my selling price made her happy? I loved my Amma and Appa; loved my Appa more than my Amma, but in some moments, some dark moments, it felt as if my Chinese mother had abandoned me without even a fleeting thought and that feeling, it fell like a hammer on my heart.

My mother's fury accelerated even as my father wearily tried to calm her down.

'She's young and stupid and that boy will make her only more headstrong. I won't let him take her away. I won't let her do it.'

'What are you talking about, Saroja? Australia will give her a whole better life, better than what she can get here.'

'She can become a teacher here.'

'Fool. Don't you know this country? She may not even get into university. You know that.'

'She can do something else. There's always something else she can do. This is all your fault. You keep giving in to her, letting her do whatever she wants.'

'You can't stop her.'

'I can. I will. We sacrificed our lives for her. She can't sacrifice hers for us?'

'You're talking rubbish now, Saroja. We don't need sacrifices like that. What kind of life is that?'

'I don't care. She's my daughter and she'll listen to me.'

'Amma!' I cried. 'I don't have money to go to Australia now. We don't even have money to pay for the cheapest college here in this country. What are you fighting about?'

'Swear to me you won't go to Australia. Swear it!'

'I won't.'

The next morning at work, my father keeled over from a heart attack.

* * *

My mother refused to leave his side at the hospital. Only one person could stay, so I left when the evening visiting hours were over.

There's a kind of exhaustion when there's a complete depletion in the body. The brain shuts down. You think you are clear-headed but you're not. You start seeing things as if you are perfectly lucid. I was having that kind of episode when I came out of the ward to the lobby where Shankar was waiting. He took one look at me and said, 'Wait for me right here. I'll go get my bike.' I waited and the lobby was emptying and it was getting dark and I was bone-weary, ravenous and there was no sign of Shankar so I walked down the path leading to the parking lot and the streetlight in that particular spot wasn't working and it felt darker than anything I'd known then a man came out of nowhere, his hand outstretched, coming at me, coming closer and closer, his voice saying, 'Missy? Missy? Hello, Miss?' and memory kicking in, I began to hyperventilate I couldn't breathe and there were yelping shrieks coming from my throat then the man ran away and Shankar was there and he got down from his bike and held me and back home, when I was still shivering and not speaking, he fed me, managing a few spoonsful before he put me to bed and while I lay on my side, he lay behind me, his arm over my waist, his body supporting my back, his head next to mine. Safe, comforted, I slept.

My father died the following evening, my mother and I by his side.

Because my father died, my mother's grief turned savage.

Because she had to pin all blame on Shankar, she told Azam's father that he had constantly harassed her husband.

Because she provided the tinder, Azam's father told his constable friend about a gangster's son who drove a poor man to his death.

Because that constable friend wanted a continued supply of free nasi lemak from his friend's wife, he told a superior about a young killer, son of a gangster with links to half the underworld.

Because that superior as a new policeman had seen a drunken gang fight on the street, and had been so terrified he had thrown up, he had a loathing of Indian thugs and wanted a chance to redeem himself.

Like a ball kicked high towards the goalpost,
all the reasons came hurtling towards us.
Because. Because. Because. Because. Because.
Because. Because. Because. Because. Because.

They came for Shankar five days after my father's funeral.
Shankar had bought dinner for everyone. Azam was whispering
to himself 'Melbourne! Melbourne! Australia! Liberty! Freedom!'

'Shush Azam,' I told him. 'Not so loud, man.' My mother was
sitting on the floor, in a corner of the room, her eyes looking at
us without expression.

Shankar went into the kitchen to wash his hands. A knock on
the open door. Two policemen stood there, pleasant but grave.
'Is Shankar Maniam here?' they asked.

'No,' I said instinctively. Azam yelled, 'Hey Shankar! Two
people to see you!' Too late, he noticed their uniforms. Too late
he noticed his father hovering in the corridor.

They said they needed to take him to the police station
for questioning regarding a death. They asked if his father was
around. Shankar protested he knew nothing about any death
except for my father's. He was shaking his head and I was trying
to tell the policemen, still polite, still pleasant, that they had made
a mistake, when I saw my mother's expression. Her face had lit
up; she had a little smile. Shankar noticed it too. 'Amma?' he cried,
his voice carrying such bleakness, such despair as if he was lost
already. Azam's father called out from the corridor, 'God is great!
God is great!' and Azam yelled at his father for the first time in his
life, 'What have you done? What have you done?'

The policemen walked Shankar out of the flat. He stopped at
the doorway and turned to me. 'Don't forget Melbourne, Janaki.'
There seemed to be a finality in his words.

'What are you saying? They just want to ask you some things,
right? You'll be back in a couple of hours. Right?' I went to him
but one of the policemen shoved me aside. I cried out and fell

down. Shankar dropped to his knees and was trying to hold me when the other policeman gave him a hard push and he went down with a thud and they were both at him and when they hauled him to his feet, his face was bloodied and they had him in handcuffs.

* * *

It took time. Everything in the bloody nightmare that followed, took time. Contacting Shankar's father when we didn't have his number. Getting it from Shankar's flat and then rushing down to the public phone booth only to find it vandalized as usual. Deciding to take a taxi instead to the nightclub where Shankar's father worked. Afterwards, Shankar's father's boss stopped him from barging into any old police station. The underworld network located where exactly Shankar was held, and following that, got the lawyers to find out what was happening. But by the time things got cleared, Shankar was dead. Perforated stomach ulcers, they said. Four days. It took four days for him to die.

* * *

Shankar's father was detained for causing a disturbance at the mortuary—he lost it, he totally, completely lost it but they let him go after a day just in time to do the last rites. The women of Melati Flats came together to wash Shankar's body, dressing him in a new white shirt and veshti. I stopped my mother from helping them. She could watch though. I made her watch. After they'd dressed Shankar, covering his body with flowers and the men laid him in the coffin, the women pushed my mother away from the flat. 'Go,' they said.

'I thought they would just rough him up a bit,' my mother wept. 'Just give him a taste of pain. I didn't think he'd die. You think I'd even have said anything if I knew?'

'You tell me,' I said, my voice pitiless.

* * *

Azam's mother, finally finding strength from where I don't know, barred his father from their flat. Azam wasn't talking to anyone, not even his mother. Since breaking down at the funeral, he'd moved inwards into near total silence.

I moved out of our flat, rented a room from a colleague. I heard that my mother's employer had offered her accommodation at the children's home. She had a buyer for our flat. Good. She wouldn't have to worry about money.

Six weeks after Shankar's death, his father dropped by to see me after school. I thought he'd be gaunt, skeletal-thin like me but for some strange reason, he looked good, even sprightly. We went to an Indian restaurant nearby and over coffee, he asked me about my plans. 'When are you going to Australia?' he asked.

'As soon as I've saved up some money, Uncle,' I said. I'd been surfing the internet in the library in our school, trying to calculate the cost of the cheapest nursing course in Australia. 'It may take some time.'

He shook his head. 'No, it doesn't have to. Here, Shankar left something for you.' He took out an official looking envelope from a bag. 'I filed the claims and they sent this to my flat. It was the only address they had for you.'

My hand shook. I didn't want to take it. 'No.'

'You have to,' he said. 'For Shankar.'

I opened the envelope and took out a letter and a cheque. It had a figure followed by too many zeros. I looked at Shankar's father. 'What's all this, Uncle?'

'Shankar took out a life insurance policy when he started working. You were the beneficiary. Listen,' he said when I tried to push the cheque towards him. 'Go to Australia. Make Shankar's dream come true.'

'This money should be yours.'

He laughed out loud, a suddenly boyish, happy smile on his face. 'I don't need the money, girl; already got plans, don't I? You just need to go get ready for Australia.'

When we left the restaurant, he held my arm. 'Janaki, you were my son's dearest friend. Thank you for that.'

I shook my head. 'I don't know how to go on, Uncle,' I whispered, my voice broken. 'I don't know what to do anymore. The teaching saves me but when it's time to go home, I have to remember to take the bus, get down at my stop, walk to my door. I have to remember to eat, to be.' My pain had settled itself like a boulder at the bottom of my heart. I knew one day, it would press down so hard, it would crack my heart.

He looked at me with Shankar's eyes and when I saw them, I began to tear up. I hadn't cried, not even at Shankar's funeral.

'Don't cry, Janaki,' he said; then of course I cried some more. He didn't seem embarrassed at all. He held me quietly.

At the last of my sniffles, he said, 'So much of pain, dear girl.'

'I hate them all for leaving. First my father, and then Shankar . . . '

He nodded. 'No time to grieve for your father before Shankar died and the way he died, dear God . . . '

I was getting weepy again. He said, 'Janaki, what are you grieving for? Their deaths? Or your loss, that you're all alone?'

I was suddenly furious. 'You think this is a big melodrama, Uncle?'

He shook his head. 'You know yourself, Janaki. You can't heal if you don't look it in the face.'

'Bloody hell,' I said. 'If I close my eyes, it's almost as if Shankar is saying those words to me.'

He smiled then, such a sad smile that I realized I'd never thought of his anguish, his pain. 'Our Shankar,' he smiled. 'Goodbye, Janaki. You know what, let the grief walk with you. Own it. Own every damn bloody bit of pain and the happiness you had too. That way, the healing may come. Or not. What do I know, I'm just bloody half-mad Indian gangster!'

He said goodbye again. As he turned to leave, I asked, 'What's your healing going to be, Uncle?'

He seemed surprised at the question. 'I didn't tell you? Making them pay, of course. People got to pay for killing my son.' He walked away waving goodbye and I distinctly heard him say 'Got a long list, girl.'

'Uncle!' I yelled. He pretended not to hear.

* * *

My mother came out of the kitchen with a bag. 'When are you leaving for Australia?'

'You know about Australia?' I asked in surprise. We had had so little conversation between us the past few months that I was only going to bring up Australia later that day.

'Everyone in Melati Flats knows about Australia. They're genuinely happy for you, you know. Gives them hope.'

I felt guilty. I'd known the folks of Melati Flats all my life but Shankar's death had erased the existence of every single person there from my memory. I was learning that grief wasn't an emotion but a state of being and in my case, I was a walking, talking shell whose insides festered with angry loss.

My mother sat on the sofa and said, 'You asked me why I hated Shankar.'

'I need to know that. To make sense of it.'

She shook her head. 'There was no reason. I hated Shankar, loathed him from the first time I saw him. That was it. We don't choose who we hate.'

'No, not true. You hated him for a reason.'

'Okay, if it makes you feel better, I could tell you that when he was a child, he kicked me and I fell. Or he stole something from me. Or I was jealous of him being so close to you. Or some nonsense like that. Or maybe in my previous birth he was my mortal enemy or something. Don't you see,' she asked me. 'I hated him—and there was no earthly reason for it.'

'Everyone else loved him.' I was childish and didn't care. 'Except you and Azam's father. Shankar could walk into any house in Melati Flats and there'd be a meal for him.'

'True.'

'And you killed him.' There. It was out. I finally said the unspoken that lay between us.

Sharp intake of breath, then she was silent for such a long time, her eyes drawn inwards, her face expressionless. I couldn't quell the gorge that rose in my throat.

'A broken jaw. Crushed ribs . . . ' I spelt out slowly.

She raised a hand to stop me. She said dully, 'A broken jaw. A bloodied nose. Black eye. Crushed ribs. Gashes on his body. Staples on his ears. Injuries on his legs, on his soles. A boy who didn't deserve to die. Who died because of me. It's the first thing I see when I wake up and the last thing when I go to sleep.'

She looked at her hands. 'I will carry that image of Shankar all the days of my life.'

It was my turn to be struck silent. How my mother had this talent to play see-saw with my feelings for her. Almost immediately, I thought how all my feelings were about me and my loss; how I felt; how I suffered; as if it was the only thing that mattered. How little had Shankar's compassion rubbed off on me.

Taking a deep breath, I said, 'You have to go away. Shankar's father . . . he has . . . '

'He has a hit list, yeah, I heard.' She looked at me. 'I don't blame him. If someone hurt my daughter I'd go after them with my parang too. Chop off their head.'

'What?'

She shook her head. 'You hate me, I know that, and I don't understand you either. We fight all the time. You are not my perfect daughter. I'm not your perfect mother. But if anyone hurts you, I'll kill them. It's like that.'

'You have to go away. Now.'

She closed her eyes. A barely perceptible shake of the head.

'Amma! Are you listening to me? Shankar's father wants you dead.'

She said softly, 'You think I'm not dead already? I died when that boy died.'

I didn't know what to say. The silence piled on between us.

Finally, I said, 'Next week. I'm going to Melbourne next week.'

'Will you take some money from the house sale?'

'No.'

She continued, 'Like a gift from your Appa. He'd like that.'

'I don't know. I'd have to think about that.'

'I'll ask the girl at the office to help me transfer the money into your account,' she said as if I hadn't spoken. 'For your Appa, Janaki. In his memory.' I looked at her and saw my mother for the first time in a long time.

I had disdained her when my friends had laughed at her, back in Standard Three. She'd been too dark, too fat, not pretty, not the right fit. To my dawning horror I realized I'd been carrying that shaming disdain ever since, subconsciously, like a badge of honour.

'I wish I'd been kinder to you,' I cried. 'I can't remember when I last hugged you, Amma—I don't even know if I can hug you now.'

'I don't think I ever hugged my mother,' she replied. 'We were not exactly a hugging family. I just obeyed her and thought my daughter would do the same—because mothers always know what's best but that's not true at all, is it? We think we do but we don't. Misplaced notions, that's what it is.'

We sat for a bit. I didn't know when I'd see my mother again. I didn't know what I was feeling towards her. 'Shall we go?' I asked. I looked around the flat. It seemed to me the ghosts were no longer sulky, just waiting.

My mother settled herself deeper into the sofa. 'You know what? You go on. I think I'll stay here a while.' She looked smaller than I ever knew her but there was a rare calm on her face.

'Okay then. I'll go first.' My words came out like little stick words. I could have stayed with her, kissed the top of her head, a bit of reconciliation and all that but that happens only in stories.

'Got to do this though, one last time.' I stood up, dropped my bag on the chair. Then I went near the TV and pushed back the coffee table to make more space. Raising my hands, I reached up, stepped one leg forward, bent down and did a perfect cartwheel.

END

14

Call It by Its Name

It was said that two hundred years ago, the British shipped Indian prisoners to this country to work in chain gangs. How dark-skinned, how scary, those prisoners. Wherever they went, the clinking sounds of their leg irons preceded them. Clink. Clink. Clink. The locals called the prisoners keling. Over time, the pejorative stretched to include all dark, scary ethnic Indians.

This evening, Mak Zah, who is my friend; who sells the crunchiest, tastiest pisang goreng this side of Kuala Lumpur; who is the bubbliest, warmest person I know—calls me keling.

It slaps my face. I have never been called keling before. Keling has always been other people.

Pak Din, her husband, who usually greets me with a smile and a joke on his lips, looks ravaged by some angry sorrow. He packs my pisang goreng in a bag, hands it to me, collects the money and retreats to the back of the stall without looking at me, without saying a single word. Mak Zah sits on a stool at the back of the stall, her hands gripping a smartphone on the table. Some preacher is peddling hate on speaker phone and he has her entire attention. I catch bits of him, reedy voice, exhorting his listeners to watch out for enemies who are planning to kill the faithful and take over the country. 'Out of sheer kindness, because we are a gentle people, because we are a good people, we allowed these people into this country. We allowed them to live, to work, to prosper but what did they do? They scorned our kindness. They took our wealth, took our lands, and now,' his voice rises in a high-pitched shriek, 'as if that isn't enough, these infidels are planning to kill us and take over the country!' Mak Zah utters furious curses under her breath.

Surely no one believes that bilge, I think—until I belatedly connect the dots. 'How are you, Mak Zah?' I call out and at once she jumps up as if on fire and cries to her husband, 'Why is that keling still here?'

Keling. I should let it go but I am rooted to the ground, too stunned to be angry. 'What did you call me, Mak Zah?' My voice is low. She looks away, her mouth set in a straight line, two spots of pink high on her cheeks. Her husband mumbles, 'Nothing, nothing, it's nothing.' He gestures with his hands for me to move along, go away and be quick about it.

Keling. I am thirty-six. Tall, slender, chocolatey-brown, educated, attractive—even exotic, if you looked at me from a certain angle. Keling has always been other people, other Indian-Malaysians; comfortable narratives to feed the disdain of other races. Keling are the darker ones. The stupid, lazy, drunk fighting-on-the-road ones. The gangsters. The drug pushers. The ones from the estates. From squatter areas. From city slums. Low life, smelly, dirty, filthy black keling. All the soothing stereotypes that exist, inexorable in the minds of others; of landlords who won't rent out to Indians; in mothers who frighten their kids with the black bogeyman. They exist in the hearts of ordinary otherwise decent folks who need someone worse off than them to feel better about their own failures and shortcomings. They need the keling.

I do not know until Mak Zah tells me, that I too am keling.

I was fourteen when I first heard a teacher use the word in class. 1982.

Form Two Hijau, the next-to-bottom class in the form. Mrs Halimah was yelling at the Indian boys. They watched her in silence, their uniforms stained with sweat, their hair combed in the actor Rajnikanth's trademark, their faces shining with contempt for her. Her list of complaints was long. They were not listening to her. They never showed her any respect. They never did their homework. They were useless, lazy fellows. They were always making a ruckus in class. She ignored the Malay boys doing exactly the same thing. The Chinese boys and all of us girls were quiet as she yelled, 'Keling! Keling! Keling! Next time, don't come to class, okay?' As she left the class, she wailed to Mr Kassim who was waiting by the door. 'I can't stand it lah, Kassim.'

Mr Kassim came in and surveyed the class. 'Let's do it this way, shall we? You are keling,' he gestured to the Indian boys. 'You,' he looked at the Malay boys. 'You are Melayu bodoh, stupid Malays, and finally,' his hands swept towards the Chinese boys. 'You are Chinese pigs. Cina babi. Okay?' His grin was infectious. There were hoots of laughter from the back of the class. 'Now that we have succeeded in insulting everyone equally, let's get this lesson going but please, don't be yelling these stupid names loudly. You want to be assholes, just yell MB, KL or CB. Understood?' We liked Mr Kassim. He was a good man. It was only years later that I realized he could say what he did only because of his race. It afforded him immunity.

I was seventeen and in the 'top' class when I realized that Lim Khong Beng, while a natural leader and the most suitable among all the prefects in school, would not be made head prefect because he was a Chinese in a Malay majority school. The headship went to Azizul who accepted it with grace. Azizul later got a government scholarship to study overseas. He is now an important figure in a government ministry. Meanwhile, after sixth form, Lim Khong Beng went to MIT to do engineering. He works in the US now, hardly ever coming back to Malaysia, not even for holidays.

I know of testimony upon testimony of such stories except that the words shift depending on who says them. One person calls it 'racial discrimination' while another swears it is 'affirmative action'. After my father died in a car crash, I applied for loans and grants to all the public and private organizations to help pay for my university fees. I was rejected repeatedly, no reason given.

Life sucked but I still had to pay fees. I tried several part-time jobs and discovered teaching tuition worked best. Another mate, Selvan, whose father was an odd-job labourer, tended bars on weekends (which was how he learned to make a mean martini. He also learned to drink gin, but that's another story.) and worked on construction sites during the long vacations to earn the fees for the following year. Occasionally, if we came early for an eight o'clock class, we would find him sleeping on a wooden bench in the Arts concourse.

While I was running around trying to get money, all my Malay university mates got scholarships, even those who wore branded outfits bought on holidays abroad. They still remained my dear friends.

I got upset but not distraught by what was happening to me. By nature, I am placid. Cowardly. Confrontation shrivels any remnant of courage in me. I normalize rejection because 'affirmative action' is something I've been used to since young. Discriminated against, denied and sidelined because of my race and religion—this doesn't desolate me even as I know the favours and opportunities are dished out to the right race. My rejections are signed off by faceless people obeying policy guidelines. I don't know the men and women who shrug off my future. They are not my friends.

But with Mak Zah, it becomes personal. We have years of friendship between us, from the time she set up the stall all those years ago. A darling woman, she looks out for all her customers. I even give her murukku and Indian sweets for Deepavali, assuring her they are all halal. She is my friend. So, like a shard of glass, the name she calls me keeps turning and twisting in my insides. After today, tomorrow, the next day, and all the days after that, Mak Zah will still be who she has always been: a good person. Except the word she uttered has disappeared all warmth and lightness in our friendship, broken us apart, so that even if we become friends again, there'll always be that crack in the cup between us. *I valued her. I thought she valued me too.*

I think to myself all friendships are transient. There's no guarantee when it comes to trust.

In the little market square off Mak Zah's, a trader and his migrant helper are dismantling their stall and packing their goods into their lorry. The helper keeps arranging the boxes wrongly. There's much pretend annoyance and scolding from the Chinese employer. He tells his dark-skinned helper, 'What is this, man? You keep doing this, you better balik India!'

The helper howls. 'How can I go back to India? I'm from Bangladesh lah!' They laugh together.

Balik India. I hear it all the time though the laughter that accompanies it is always mocking, not amusing. I am ethnic Indian. I have never been to India. How can I go *back* to a country I've never been to? My great grandfather arrived in Malaya when he was four. My grandfather was born here; my father and I, too. When does an immigrant cease to be an immigrant in this land? Not ever, if his ancestors came from China or India.

My friend Viji told me of her ten-day package tour to South India. 'Everything they say about India in the ads—you know *Incredible India,* etc. is totally true. The temples, the shopping— oh my God—the food! I loved everything. It was my heritage after all, except . . . ' she paused. 'It wasn't home. I'm not *Indian* Indian, you know what I mean?' she asked and I nodded. 'I didn't belong, but it didn't matter. When I came back home, I dashed to the nearest Chinese restaurant to have char kuay teow.' We both laughed. 'Ethnic and cultural Indian with a Malaysian operating system and apps . . . ' she said. I knew what she meant.

I pass by Uncle Shamsuddin's shop on my way to the LRT station to take the train home. He works for a man who rents half a shop lot to sell toys. Uncle Shamsuddin, my father's neighbour, and one of his numerous Malay friends when they were growing up, was part of my childhood too. I hand him the pisang goreng.

'Girl,' he beams. 'So nice of you!'

'Not really lah, Uncle.'

Back home it's too humid to have tea. I grab a beer and lean back on the rattan chair in the porch. The beer reminds me of Mitch, my American friend. We're in the same writing circle. Mitch peppers his sentences with 'lah' as condiment. He loved his beer but stopped drinking completely when he converted to marry his Malay girlfriend. Mitch thinks that his marriage makes him an expert on all things Malay. He once pointed to a news report about an argument escalating on social media because of the word keling. 'Such a fuss,' Mitch shook his head. 'Keling is just a word to describe Indian Malaysians lah. My wife says that actually, keling was a term of respect, honour even, to describe the Kalinga people centuries ago. It isn't derogatory at all.'

'Fine, Mitch,' I said. 'I take it if you meet an African American, you'll have no problem calling him the N-word, right?'

'Whoa! Wait a minute!' He jumped up from his chair. 'I'll never use that word anywhere to anybody. That's sick.' His face turned brick red. I said nothing. 'That's how it is with this K-word too?

'What do you think?'

'I'm sorry. I didn't realize.' He struggled with himself. 'I'm sure my wife didn't know . . . ' He stopped. He was too honest to deny that perhaps his wife had said exactly what she had wanted him to believe. Of all the origin stories of 'keling', the most scurrilous is the one about the noble Kalinga kingdom and how its people were called Kalinga which became 'keling' over the centuries. It is like being given a pat on the back before being told, 'Yeah, I know what I'm doing when I call you a stupid dumb-fuck but don't worry, "dumb-fuck" used to be an honourable name.'

My friends who've migrated to the UK and US tell me to join them abroad. 'Discrimination here isn't legislated by law,' they say. One of them, Freddie, told me of the fun they have together as former Malaysians. 'Every year, on Merdeka Day, August 31, we gather in my house for a party. It's potluck with nasi lemak, rendang, roti canai, the whole works. We sing the national anthem—hey, I still remember the words—and then someone puts on a CD of P. Ramlee's songs. We dance the joget—all wrong steps—and talk of the lives we've left behind, friends, family, neighbours, places. Complete nostalgia of course,' He laughed at the thought. 'You can say we celebrate a place which doesn't exist anymore except as a hole in our belly.'

Later that night after several glasses of gin and tonic, he confessed, 'I told you about our annual Merdeka Day bash, right? There's more. Something else dances alongside us and eats the food and shades our stories.'

'You're creeping me out, Freddie!'

'Nah,' he raised his glass. 'That thing isn't a ghost. I think it's our resentment. We had to leave our country to make a life for ourselves. You know the reasons why. Everyone knows the effing affirmative-action-new-economic-policy reasons why. But. It. Still. Hurts. Because your country's saying *get lost, and good riddance.* We're not a loss at all.' Ten years in Glasgow, ten happy rewarding years there and Freddie still bled afresh each time he came back to Malaysia.

* * *

I live alone. A gardener takes care of the garden where my mother spent all her waking hours when she was alive. She planted the two frangipani trees that stand sentinel by the gate overriding neighbours' protests that they were cemetery trees. Grey bark, sparse, gnarled branches, one tree sprouting yellow blooms, the other white, both heady with fragrance. By the steps leading to the porch, she fixed a stone jar and threw some lotus seeds in the water. Now, lazy goldfish swim in circles in the water where a lone lotus rises, pink with exertion. She planted marigolds, tulasi, sunflowers, tomatoes, long beans, okra, deliberately mixing the flowers and vegetables in the same raised beds.

The arrangement was penance for the times she created a fuss when my father, a factory manager, brought some of his workers home for lunch. She'd grumble. 'Who are these people? I don't know their race, their religion, their caste . . . What plates will I set out? Eversilver or ceramic?'

My father would tell her to set out the type we used every day, our eversilver plates. 'Every village is my village. Every man, my kin,' he'd quote from a Tamil poem written 2000 years ago. He lived by the message. My mother couldn't.

As I sit and remember, my silly dog Earl Grey, who thinks he is a cat, keeps brushing against my legs before he decides he'd teased me enough. He strolls to the stone bench in the garden to stretch out in the sun.

In the soft darkening of the evening, the garden carries the scent of a summer poem. By turns, peaceful and riotous, slumbering yet alert, the garden tells me keling and all sorts of name-calling are sacrilegious in this space. Then of course, I think of what Mitch mentioned once. 'I know what the Chinese and Indians call the Malays. They've said it to me to my face, not knowing I'm married to one.'

'Bloody hell, how awful for you, Mitch,' I replied. 'Every blinking race in this country does that. Every bloody one.' He nodded.

No one says it out aloud but it's there, all right. Behind all the politeness, and all the bowing and smiling, all of us, we carry our assumptions of our own superiority and other people's worthlessness on our heads until our necks break from the sheer weight.

I'm afraid of shadows. I'm afraid of the strange silhouettes that dance in the dark. I'm afraid of creepy sounds, rustles, swishes that I can't identify. Everything looks and sounds macabre in the creeping gloom. Courage is not my middle name. I never sit in the porch at night. Today, I do. I'm still afraid but don't make a move to go inside. Earl Grey jumps into my lap and as I scratch his ears, a profound grief washes over me.

I'm grieving. The grief bleeds inside my body. I loved Mak Zah. She hurled a slur at me. I'm raging at her now. What if Uncle Shamsuddin calls me by a racist name? Will I hate him too? How capricious everything is.

Hate feels comfortable, a nurturing place to be in when the hater is a victim. I don't want to be a victim. I don't want to dine out on my displacement in my own country. I don't want my life to be a banality of hate and despair, regret and nostalgia. I don't want to open the door to those beasts but I don't know how not to. I sit and be. Earl Grey licks my hand. I see the shadows in the garden, monstrous, menacing, skulking and sneaking up on me. The scent of the frangipani wafts in the air. In the darkness I strain to see the lotus in the stone jar by the foot of the steps to the porch.

END

Acknowledgements

My deepest appreciation and gratitude to Sharon Bakar, my friend and first writing coach, who not only believed in my stories, but constantly encouraged, supported and pushed this book into becoming.

The Prague Summer Program for Writers (PSP) shaped me as a writer. I am indebted beyond measure to Richard Katrovas for generously giving me space at the PSP, not once but several times. Thank you as well, Richard and Stu Dybek, for the most transformative coaching and writing perspectives. Attending the PSP was always like coming home to family.

To the international writers' residence, Le Chateau de Lavigny: I was raw, unpublished but you saw me as a writer and invited me to Switzerland, based solely on work I submitted to you. I will always remember. Thank you.

My thanks to Raman Krishnan of Silverfish who first published my stories, not counting those published when I was an undergrad. To Word Works and the DK Dutt Award for Literary Excellence, thank you.

Danton Remoto insisted that I knocked on the door, and Nora Nazerene Abu Bakar not only opened it but welcomed me in. Thank you both. Thank you too to the indefatigable Ishani Bhattacharya.

And thank you, Kannan-Sithambaram and Nagappan, who have always been there.

Permissions and Credits

1   The stanza, 'Nothing is more enduring' in "**When I Speak of Kuala Lumpur**" is an English translation of the first stanza of the poem 'Hujan Bulan Juni' by Sapardi Djoko Damono, from the poetry collection of the same title, first published by Gramedia Pustaka Utama. Translated by Saras Manickam with permission from Ibu Sonya Sondakh, copyright holder of the author's estate.

2   'Dey Raju' first appeared in *Silverfish New Writing 6*; Silverfish Books, 2006 (ISBN 983-3221-12-2)

3   'Invisible' first appeared in *Silverfish New Writing 7*; Silverfish Books, 2008 (ISBN 978-983-3221-20-2)

4   'It's All Right, Auntie' first appeared in *Readings from Readings: New Malaysian Writing*, Word Works, 2011 (ISBN 978-967-10292-0-6)

5   'Will You Let Him Drink The Wind?' first appeared in *Readings from Readings 2: New Malaysian Writing*; Word Works, 2012 (ISBN 978-967-10292-1-3)

    A French version of the story, 'Le Laisserez-vous Boire le Vent?' translated by Brigitte Bresson, appeared in the publication, *Jentayu revue Littéraire d'Asie*, Numéro 10 – Été 2019

6   'The Princess of Lumut' first appeared in *Champion Fellas*, Word Works, 2016 (ISBN 978-967-10292-2-0). It was a runner-up in the 2015 DK Dutt Memorial Award for Literary Excellence. This version has been slightly revised.

7 'Charan' won the first prize in the 2017 DK Dutt Memorial Award for Literary Excellence. It first appeared in *Endings & Beginnings*, Word Works, 2018 (ISBN 978-967-10292-5-1). 'Charan' also appeared in *Ronggeng-Ronggeng: Malaysian Short Stories*, Maya Press, 2020 (ISBN 978-983-2737-59-9).

8 'My Mother Pattu' won the regional prize for Asia in the 2019 Commonwealth Short Story Prize. It first appeared online in *Granta* in 2019. In 2021, it was published in *The Art and Craft of Asian Stories*, Bloomsbury, 2021 (ISBN 978-1-350-07654-9). It was also featured in *The Best Malaysian Stories 2021-2020* (ISBN: 978-967-16599-4-6).

9 An early version of 'Woman in the Mirror' first appeared in the March 29, 2020 online edition of the *Business Mirror*, Philippines.

10 'When I Speak of Kuala Lumpur' was shortlisted for the Master's Review Summer Short Story Award, 2021.

11 'When We are Young' first appeared in *Unsaid*, Penguin Random House SEA, 2022 (IBSN: 9789815017090)